Praise for the Neil Flambé Capers

"Good fun."—celebrity chef Gordon Ramsey

"This would be a great book-club choice. Participants could create the perfect seven-course meal as an accompaniment to discussing such an engaging and lively read."
—*School Library Journal*

"A giggle from beginning to end."   —CM *Magazine*

"The constant suspense, innocent romance, a lovely recipe for scones, and the flamboyant, irrepressible chef will captivate fans of the series and impel new readers to the nearest bookstore or library."   —*Kirkus Reviews*

Also by Kevin Sylvester

Neil Flambé

and the
DUEL IN THE DESERT

KEVIN
SYLVESTER

Simon & Schuster Books for Young Readers
New York   London   Toronto   Sydney   New Delhi

SIMON & SCHUSTER BOOKS FOR YOUNG READERS

An imprint of Simon & Schuster Children's Publishing Division

1230 Avenue of the Americas, New York, New York 10020

This book is a work of fiction. Any references to historical events, real people, or real places are used fictitiously. Other names, characters, places, and events are products of the author's imagination, and any resemblance to actual events or places or persons, living or dead, is entirely coincidental.

Copyright © 2016 by Kevin Sylvester

All rights reserved, including the right of reproduction in whole or in part in any form.

SIMON & SCHUSTER BOOKS FOR YOUNG READERS

is a trademark of Simon & Schuster, Inc.

For information about special discounts for bulk purchases, please contact Simon & Schuster Special Sales at 1-866-506-1949 or business@simonandschuster.com.

The Simon & Schuster Speakers Bureau can bring authors to your live event. For more information or to book an event, contact the Simon & Schuster Speakers Bureau at 1-866-248-3049 or visit our website at www.simonspeakers.com.

Also available in a Simon & Schuster Books for Young Readers hardcover edition

Book design by Laurent Linn and Tom Daly

The text for this book was set in Goudy Old Style.

The illustrations for this book were rendered in pen and ink.

Manufactured in the United States of America

0117 OFF

First Simon & Schuster Books for Young Readers paperback edition February 2017

2 4 6 8 10 9 7 5 3 1

The Library of Congress has cataloged the hardcover edition as follows:

Sylvester, Kevin, author, illustrator.

Neil Flambé and the duel in the desert / Kevin Sylvester.

pages cm. — (The Neil Flambé capers ; 6)

Summary: Neil and his friend Larry travel in their new food truck to the Salsa Verde ranch in Arizona to participate in the legendary food-truck gathering, but when Neil discovers that the Verde ranch is in danger of foreclosure, the only hope for the ranch is a treasure map left behind by the very first Verde, a chef who discovered a mine while escaping from a murderous army colonel.

ISBN 978-1-4814-1041-0 (hardback)

ISBN 978-1-4814-1042-7 (pbk)

ISBN 978-1-4814-1043-4 (eBook)

[1. Mystery and detective stories. 2. Cooking—Fiction. 3. Food trucks—Fiction. 4. Treasure maps—Fiction. 5. Ranch life—Fiction.] I. Title. II. Title: Duel in the desert.

PZ7.S98348Nek 2016

[Fic]—dc23

2015019404

To the Berot-Burns family—
partners in adventure!

CHAPTER ONE

BORDER CROSS

Neil could see the look of shock on the border guard's face before they reached the inspection booth.

"This is not going to go well," Neil muttered. Larry slammed on the brakes, which let out an earsplitting squeal with a side order of blue smoke and a soupçon of burning rubber. Neil's head whipped forward, then snapped back.

"On the contrary, it's going AWESOME!" Larry said.

Neil caught a glimpse of the guard through Larry's window. She had her eyes closed and her hands clapped tightly over her ears. She was frowning.

Larry turned off the ignition, let out a giant "WHOOP!" and began playing an imaginary drum solo on the steering wheel.

The guard coughed and waved the smoke away. She leaned out of her kiosk, taking in the length and height of the strange vehicle that had just appeared in front of her.

She gave her head a bewildered shake.

Larry smiled and winked at Neil. "I think she's impressed with the FrankenWagon."

"Ugh."

The FrankenWagon was the new Flambé food truck, and Neil hated it. It was a hybrid in the same way chicken-chocolate ice cream is a hybrid. It was welded together from an old Volkswagen van at the front and a silver Airstream trailer at the back. There was a visible welding line that ran around the entire cab, like a scar, and Neil was sure it was going to split apart every time they turned a corner.

The guard narrowed her eyes and growled.

"I don't think 'impressed' is the right word," Neil said, secretly wishing that border guards had their kiosks on the passenger side.

"Open the window!" the woman bellowed.

Larry smiled and pointed his finger in the air in the universal sign for *wait a second.*

"NOW!"

Larry nodded. Neil watched as Larry used an electric mixer to quickly roll down the window. He'd had to lean down to plug the mixer into the makeshift socket he'd installed in the dashboard, and it looked very suspicious, Neil realized, like maybe Larry was hiding something quickly at his feet.

The window lowered slowly, slowly, and Neil was sure he saw the guard reach for her weapon.

"Where are your hands?" the guard demanded.

Larry raised them, still holding the mixer.

"Pretty sweet, eh?" he said. "I made that myself after the original handle broke off."

She frowned. A bead of sweat ran down Neil's forehead.

"Passports," said the guard.

Larry leaned on the door frame. "No worries. My cousin will just fetch them from yonder glove compartment. Speaking of fetching . . . may I get a name to put to the lovely face and oh-so-fetching uniform?"

The guard stayed stone-faced. Neil had seen Larry's charm work on all sorts of people, but the border guard seemed immune.

Neil grabbed the passports and leaned past Larry to hand them to the woman.

She snatched them from his hands.

"Dolores?" Larry asked.

She ignored him and stared at the passport photos.

"Petunia?"

"Where are you heading?" she said, gliding the passports under some kind of scanner. Larry's passport set off a series of beeps, and the guard's eyes grew wide as she gazed at her computer screen.

"That depends, Marilyn?"

"Depends?"

"Arizona!" Neil yelled, squeezing his head through Larry's window. "We're heading down to Arizona for a couple of weeks for a food convention."

"The Broiling Man Festival. Heard of it?" Larry said, smiling.

"In *this*?" She snorted, her professional demeanor momentarily broken by disbelief. "Good luck."

"So we're clear to go?" Larry said.

She went back to staring at her beeping computer screen.

Neil wanted to slide down his seat and disappear through the floor of the FrankenWagon. Something, he thought sadly, that was probably all too possible. Larry had already warned him against moving the foot carpets.

The interrogation continued.

The guard asked if the FrankenWagon was legal. Larry responded with a thumbs-up. "Legal and awesome!" Neil banged his forehead on the dashboard.

"Can you prove it?" she said.

"You want to take it for a spin?"

She growled.

Neil quickly grabbed the permits and registration for the vehicle from the glove compartment and lunged past Larry, who was still trying to make googly eyes at the guard.

She asked if they had a visa to work in the States, since this was "allegedly a food truck."

"Is it really work when cooking is your *passion?*" Larry said, leaning his head further out the window.

Neil scrambled to pass over the official invitation to the festival.

All this time, the computer continued to beep.

Larry began to sing the song "Home on the Range" to the beat, doing strange robot motions with his arms.

"I know," Larry said, his arms rotating. "I'll call you DoloroLynPetunia."

DoloroLynPetunia had had enough. She handed them back the pass- ports and ordered them to go to a large building to their left.

"Did we win something?" Larry asked.

Neil smacked his face into his palm.

DoloroLynPetunia pointed with more force.

"Is that where we claim the prize?" Larry beamed, turning the key and firing up the FrankenWagon.

DoloroLynPetunia responded with one more emphatic point of her finger toward the building. "Secondary inspection. Now."

Neil foresaw doom.

If they were lucky, they'd only be trapped at the border for a few hours.

If they were unlucky, they'd be sent packing back home and told not to come back, possibly forever.

Neil lowered his head into his hands and moaned.

"Oh, give me a home where the cantaloupes roam!" Larry sang as he happily steered the truck toward the secondary inspection building.

Maybe if Neil could talk to the officer first, if he could explain that Larry was odd, but safe. He put his hand on the door handle and prepared to leap out as soon as they parked.

A large man pointed to a parking space in front of the building and then held up his hand in a *stop* sign as Larry flew into the spot.

Neil was out in a flash and ran to the front of the truck first. He realized immediately that rushing a border officer, even with the best of intentions, was not a good idea.

The officer reached for his gun and yelled, "HALT!"

Neil screeched to a stop. The officer looked Neil up and down and frowned.

"It's a bit early for Halloween, isn't it?" he said.

Neil was wearing his chef's outfit. It had been the only clean thing in his room when they'd left that morning.

Neil heard a click as Larry opened his door and stepped out. Neil winced.

A flippered foot gingerly felt for the ground.

The guard's eyes grew wide.

Something resembling a shaggy blond dog had stepped out of the driver's-side door. It was wearing scuba gear.

The guard glanced back and forth from the redhead in the chef outfit to the goofball in scuba gear and controlled his jaw muscles enough to utter one word.

"Strip."

CHAPTER TWO

NOT HOME, AND
RANGING

Seven hours later they were back on the road. Neil refused to sit up front with Larry. Instead he was at the very back of the trailer, leaning on the stove. After being interrogated for an hour in a freezing-cold room, they'd been forced to open up every single one of their containers. They were in such a hurry to get away that Neil wasn't 100 percent sure they'd crammed everything back in. But he was 99 percent sure that what they had repacked was swaying dangerously as Larry maneuvered the FrankenWagon onto the highway.

"Slow down!" Neil called out, clutching the edge of the stove for balance.

"It's all good, chef boy!"

"Is it? Because your crazy driving is what got Dolorolunatica, or whatever her name was, mad at us in the first place! Then the Hulk saw you in your scuba gear—"

"And you in your Halloween outfit."

"AND MADE ME STRIP DOWN TO MY UNDERWEAR!"

"You shouldn't have worn the boxers with the cupcakes on them." Larry chuckled, which only made Neil more furious. "Look, chef boy, I wasn't the one who tried to smuggle Angel's sausages into the country."

Neil frowned. His culinary mentor, Angel Jícama, had given Neil some of the most sublime sausages Neil had ever smelled. He'd almost cried as the customs officer had packed them in a plastic bag and thrown them into a garbage can labeled BANNED.

"That was supposed to be dinner tonight," Neil said, frowning. "And anyway, you're the one with the passport of a thousand beeps!"

Larry gunned the engine in response. Neil listened for the sound of sirens following them.

"Not one of those beeps got us deported," Larry called back. "So I can only assume they were alerting

the border patrol to how astounding I am. Each beep was probably just a point on the sliding scale of Larry-tastic."

"I think that wet suit is cutting off the oxygen to your brain."

Larry responded by staring into the rearview mirror and sucking in his cheeks to look like a fish.

Neil rolled his eyes.

The scuba gear.

Neil had refused to allow Larry to take up any packing space for something so stupid, so Larry had insisted on wearing the gear for the trip.

"I snuck in an extra scuba outfit for you, too," Larry said. "I had to leave behind some stuff that looked like flour."

"What!?! That was my premixed bannock!"

Larry swerved and honked, and as if on cue, an extra oxygen tank slipped out from somewhere between the boxes and slammed into Neil's foot.

"Why do we need scuba gear IN THE DESERT?" Neil yelled, jumping up and down and grabbing his throbbing toes.

"Gotta be prepared for anything," Larry answered.

Neil racked his brain for any possible "anything" that could require a wet suit and oxygen in one-hundred-degree cactus-loving weather.

"You're an idiot," he said.

"You know, it's actually way more stable up here at the front," Larry called. "I'd hate to see us get a ticket because you're not wearing a seat belt."

"I think it's safer back here, thanks," Neil said.

Larry swerved again, and a box of Neil's signature

spice rub slipped from its perch and crashed onto Neil's head. Chili powder exploded in an ocher cloud, stinging his eyes. His feet hurt. His head now hurt, and he could barely see.

"You sure?" Larry called.

"Argh." Neil gritted his teeth and slowly limped his way up the narrow path between the boxes and sat down in the passenger seat. Neil took Larry's water bottle and splashed his eyes.

"I'm still mad at you," Neil said, wiping his face with his sleeve.

"Status quo!" Larry looked at him and smiled. "Hey, look. This is an adventure, so not everything's gonna go smoothly."

"You do realize we've *never* had an adventure that went smoothly *at all*."

"Seems like the best kind of adventure for a chef . . . choppy!" Larry said.

Neil rolled his eyes. "How much longer before we get there?"

"What are you, three? Did you also remember to go wee-wee before we left the border?"

"I'm just trying to figure how late we'll be thanks to our *choppy* experience at the border."

"Well, the FrankenWagon here isn't necessarily built for speed."

"Or for humans."

"But if I can find enough stops for coffee on the road, I can drive for hours, and we should get there in a couple of days. Give or take a day if I have to drive off the main highway looking for *good* coffee."

Neil slumped down in his seat and rubbed the bump on his head. "I'm going to nap. If I go into a coma, wake me when we get there."

Larry sipped his coffee and chuckled.

"There" was the Salsa Verde Ranch. Neil had been invited by the owners, Julio Verde and his daughter Feleena, for the Broiling Man Festival, an annual week-long bonfire and barbecue bonanza. Food trucks from all over North America were on their way to the ranch. Larry was, in his own words, *stoked*.

Neil wasn't as stoked, much as he looked forward to winning whatever prizes were going to be handed out for best chef, best ribs, best food truck. He had even cleared a space in his bedroom to hold all the medals he'd be bringing back.

But glory wasn't the real reason for the trip. Truth was, Neil needed a break. And he was hoping a trip to Salsa Verde would give it to him.

Angel Jícama had stayed at Salsa Verde years before, in the midst of the roughest patch of his life. After a duel had gone horribly wrong, leaving another chef dead, Angel had quit cooking, roaming the world aimlessly. He'd arrived at the front gate to Salsa Verde barely alive, and had been invited to stay.

Angel often said that the peace and relaxation he'd felt at the ranch had saved him and set him back on the path to recovery.

Neil was definitely in need of recovery. His restaurant, Chez Flambé, was being demolished even as he and Larry drove down the highway.

Chez Flambé was a dump, as Neil had proclaimed

often, but it had been his dump. His little place of food prep perfection. And, if he had to admit it, it was his home.

With no warning the city had taken it away. They were building a new road, and Chez Flambé was in the way. End of story.

Neil and Larry had salvaged everything they could, but it wasn't much. The building itself was in a bad part of town, so the compensation from the city was small.

The money wasn't that important to Neil, not really. The demolition was just one more indignation, one more blow to his dreams.

After the city told him the bad news, Neil had just stayed in his room, hiding under his covers and refusing to talk to anyone. His girlfriend, Isabella Tortellini, had tried to get Neil to snap out of his funk. So had Police Inspector Sean Nakamura, Neil's parents, and Larry. Larry had even held an all-night karaoke of Ramones songs in the hallway.

Neil had lodged a number of forks and knives into the door on his side, but even Larry's falsetto version of "I Wanna Be Sedated" hadn't lured Neil, tempted as he was, to kill Larry in person.

Finally Angel had broken through with a bribe, of sorts.

Angel snuck a thin slice of beef under Neil's door, a cut of beef more sublime than the rarest, most expensive *wagyu*.

Neil smelled it and sat bolt upright.

Angel had attached a note to the beef. *Want to know where this comes from? OPEN THE DOOR!*

Neil opened his door.

It had come from Salsa Verde.

Larry had taken what little money they had and had bought the trailer and van that had become the FrankenWagon. Neil had taken his favorite ovens, deep fryers, pots, and pans and retrofitted them as best he could to the cramped conditions of the trailer.

And now they were on the road, driving toward a future Neil felt he could no longer predict.

He closed his eyes and let the rhythm of the road lull him to sleep.

CHAPTER THREE

RANCH DRESSING

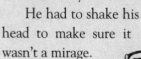alsa Verde Ranch loomed in the distance, like an oasis. The FrankenWagon had passed through hours of desert, scraggly bush, and large saguaro cacti. Then they'd begun driving down a long slope, into a sheltered valley.

"The valley is actually a gigantic crater," Larry said. "It was caused, like, a gazillion years ago when some asteroid smashed into the earth."

Neil nodded but wasn't really interested. He was more taken by what he saw.

He had to shake his head to make sure it wasn't a mirage.

It wasn't.

Luscious green and golden fields seemed to roll on forever. The side of the crater rose up all around, forming a natural border. Cattle, sheep, and chickens roamed freely, and fruit and nut trees swayed in the breeze. Neil stuck his nose out of the window and took a deep breath. It smelled amazing.

There was still zero chance of needing scuba gear. Neil looked at Larry, who had stowed the gear in the stove and changed into shorts and a T-shirt.

(Actually, a me-shirt—one of Larry's many inventions—an inside-out shirt that said COWBOY? NO. COWMAN! At least that was what Larry said it said.)

They passed under a large wooden gate and drove down the winding road toward the ranch house. Larry's screeching brakes announced their arrival.

Neil got out of the truck and stood on the driveway. He couldn't hear anything but the sound of the breeze and the distant mooing of the cows. The pebbles shuffled slightly under his feet. The breeze ruffled his red hair as he took in the Salsa Verde ranch house. Angel had talked about how odd and quirky it was.

The main entrance of the house was adobe, with the ends of huge timber beams sticking out. The wood was weathered and cracked. It must have been a hundred years old.

A whole grove of olive trees, some tall, some small, provided shade for the porch, which ran the entire length of the first floor. There was a newer addition that included a second floor and a stone-and-timber house that was wider and apparently much longer than the original part. It reminded Neil of a well-executed

FrankenWagon, but without the worry it would collapse at any moment.

The carved oak door opened and Julio Verde bounded to meet them, a huge smile on his tanned face. His hair and mustache were as silver as a sardine's skin.

"¡Hola! Welcome to my beautiful ranch," he said, shaking Neil's hand. "You may stay here for as long as you wish, but Angel says I must order you to cook your wonderful potatoes!"

Neil smiled. "Not a problem."

Larry ran up to them. "Hola, Señor Verde. ¿Cómo estás?"

"¡No me puedo quejar! ¿Y usted?"

"¡Bien, gracias, amigo!"

"Mucho gusto, Larry, nice to meet you," Julio said, shaking his hand vigorously. "There is already fresh coffee waiting in the sunroom."

Tears of joy began to well in Larry's eyes, and he rushed toward the house and the waiting caffeine.

The door creaked and a young woman walked out, dressed in jeans, boots, and a checked shirt. Larry stopped in his tracks.

"Ah! May I introduce my daughter, Feleena," Verde said. "Feleena, this is Neil Flambé."

"Hi," Neil said, waving awkwardly. He knew there was a daughter, but Feleena was completely different from the image he'd had. Angel had described playing hide-and-seek with a little girl, so Neil was taken aback to see a young woman. But of course she was a woman. Angel had been here years ago.

"And this is his cousin, Larry."

"*Hola, señorita*," Larry said, through his goofy grin. Neil could see Larry wrestling with himself. Coffee? Or stay here and get to know Feleena better? The indecision kept him rooted to the spot, swaying like the olive trees.

"Nice to meet you both," she said with a smile and a slight nod of her head. "*Papá*, I'm just going to check on the horses." She gave her father a peck on the cheek. "I will be back for dinner. I understand we are having potatoes." She gave Neil a glowing smile and a wink, and then walked away.

Larry watched her for a bit, still speechless, then shook his head and made a beeline for the coffee smell that wafted out from the house.

"She reminds me so much of her late mother," Verde said, a sad look in his eyes.

"I'm very sorry," Neil said. Angel had mentioned Señora Verde. She'd died of cancer a few years before.

Julio gave a deep sigh. "If it were not for my daughter, and my home, I do not think I could have survived. This place does have, as I'm sure Angel mentioned, a supernatural calming effect."

Neil nodded. "He called it a 'place to heal, to find comfort, to find yourself.'"

Julio smiled. "Yes. This is thanks to Mother Nature, not to me. But we have done what we can to build a home to match the natural beauty. Shall we?" Verde said, gesturing for Neil to follow Larry into the house.

The house was even more impressive on the inside. Hand-hewn beams supported the ceiling of the entrance-way, not far from the top of Neil's head.

"This original house was built by the first Verde to settle here on the ranch, more than a hundred years ago. Small meant cool, and it does get very hot here in Arizona, as you well know. Thankfully, we have modern technology today to keep us comfortable. We have been able to expand."

The back wall of the original house had been broken through to make an entrance into the addition beyond.

"Whoa," Neil said as Verde led him into the spacious living room.

Everything was wood, stone, and glass. Floor-to-ceiling windows looked out on a vista of fields and distant mountains. The chairs were leather and wood. The floors were covered with woven carpets in reds, oranges, and browns.

At the end of the main room was an enormous stone fireplace. Larry was slumped in a chair by the stone hearth, sipping his coffee and sighing contentedly.

"Fireplace?" Neil said. He thought of how hot the last day of driving had been as they'd gone through Nevada and Arizona. Larry had not, much to Neil's chagrin, outfitted the FrankenWagon with a working air conditioner.

"It can get *very* cold in the night. In the desert there is no humidity to trap heat, so it can be brutally hot at noon and close to freezing at midnight. We will very likely need a fire later tonight, in fact. But for now, it is hot. Would you care for something cool to drink?"

"Yes, please," Neil said, distracted by something mounted on the chimney over the mantel. A large wooden frame that seemed to be empty.

Neil walked over. It wasn't empty. Instead the frame contained a small piece of paper, with some numbers and pictures scrawled on it in a kind of red ink. The edges seemed to be singed. Neil squinted but couldn't make out the details. The frame itself was made from weathered scraps of wood, tacked together with rusty nails.

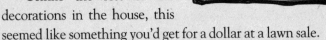

Unlike the rest of the decorations in the house, this seemed like something you'd get for a dollar at a lawn sale.

Julio walked back into the room carrying two chilled glasses.

"Ah, I see you have spotted our family heirloom," Verde said.

"What is it, exactly?" Neil asked.

"A map."

"Map?" Neil gulped. He had a sinking feeling in the pit of his stomach. Why were there always maps? Maps always led to some kind of mystery that would get him shot at or beaten up.

"Yes, but alas, a map to nowhere," Verde said, offering Neil a cool lemonade. Neil didn't even need to sip it to know it was made with lemons from the ranch. They smelled almost sweet, with a honey overtone that cut through the acidity. Sipping the drink confirmed how wonderful it was.

"To nowhere?" Neil asked. He hoped that meant it was also useless.

Verde gave an enigmatic smile. "Feleena will explain more tomorrow at the festival. Let's just say that it has sentimental value, but no monetary value, sadly." Neil thought he saw Julio wince, as if he were in pain, but then Julio lifted his head and smiled again. "The paper is very old, I can tell you that."

"The frame seems kind of, I don't know . . ."

"Like I found it in a dump?"

Neil nodded.

Verde laughed. "Yes, it appears so, but the frame is actually made of wood from the original barn that stood just outside here. A fire burned it to the ground. So many of the cattle we housed there for the winter were burned alive."

"I'm very sorry." Neil thought of the amazing beef the ranch produced.

Verde smiled. "Ah, that was very long ago, when I was just a boy."

Neil pointed at the singed edges of the map. "So the map was stored in the barn?"

Julio shook his head. "It had been kept in the house, always. But when the fire was extinguished, the map was discovered in the debris, inside an iron box. How it got there is a bit of a mystery, actually."

Neil almost spat out the lemonade at the word "mystery" but kept it together. He had spent most of the past two years trying to juggle life as a chef, student, and globe-trotting supersleuth. It was not a juggling act he enjoyed. He decided to change the subject quickly. He had come here to recuperate, not be a detective.

"I'm wondering if I can see the kitchen."

"Of course! I imagine you are eager to get back to cooking after all that time on the road. To practice for the festival!"

"Definitely." Neil smiled and followed Verde into the kitchen. There, waiting for him on the counter, by some miracle, was Neil's most cherished ingredient— potatoes from his friend Ming's private garden.

CHAPTER FOUR

DONUT FENCE
ME IN

Neil woke up refreshed. Hummingbirds were whizzing back and forth among the rosemary and honeysuckle outside his window. A gentle breeze carried the smells of flowers, herbs, and grass. He could smell hay and immediately started working out a recipe for a burned hay ice cream that would be smoky, but also sweet. It was all starting to come back, his love for great cuisine.

It had cooled down so much that Neil had needed a blanket in the middle of the night, just the way he liked it. He hadn't slept so well in months. Angel was right. This was a place to heal.

His phone buzzed. It was a text from Isabella.

How is my favorite chef doing?

Neil smiled and texted back, *I'm great!*

The phone buzzed.

I meant Larry.

Neil frowned. His phone buzzed again.

But I'm happy my second-favorite chef is also doing well.

Ha-ha! Neil typed. *Larry keeps calling this place Rivendell, whatever that means.*

From The Hobbit.

Oh. Is that a cookbook?

It was a while before the phone buzzed again.

You were supposed to read it in English class.

Oh.

Must run. Getting ready for big show. Jones says hi.

Have a good one!

Neil sighed. Isabella would love Salsa Verde. But she was getting ready for a huge perfume convention in Argentina, and there was no time for any side trips.

His phone buzzed again. It was from Jones, Isabella's bodyguard.

Jones does not say hi.

Some things never change, Neil thought. He and Jones had helped save each other during their recent trip to London, but Jones still seemed to hope he and Isabella would split.

There was a knock at the door, and Larry peeped his head inside Neil's room.

"Rise and shine, chef boy!"

"You just up or still up?" Neil asked, sliding off the bed.

"Does it matter? There's a coffee aroma floating up from the kitchen and, I hope, the Verdes awaiting to let us know what this Broiling Man is all about."

Neil nodded. The Broiling Man Festival was still a bit of a mystery to him. He'd asked Larry about the rules more than a few times, and Larry had always responded with a shrug, "I'm not a hundred percent sure. I think we find out the details when we get down there. I do know it's supposed to be AMAZING!"

The contest rules didn't really matter, of course. Neil had been in all sorts of competitions and duels, and he'd always won. He just wanted *some* idea of what he should prepare.

The thought of fighting a cooking duel again made his fingers tingle. He'd repeatedly promised Isabella he would stop fighting food duels. Duels between chefs were part of the underbelly of the world of high cuisine. She had lost her father in a duel that had gone horribly wrong. The same duel that had sent Angel into exile, and led him to Salsa Verde Ranch.

Neil had told Isabella he only did it for the money, or as part of his detective work, but he knew that wasn't totally true. He loved the thrill. He needed it. He also needed to win, to show the world that he wasn't just some kid with a cooking hobby, but the world's greatest chef.

Neil took a deep breath. He was starting to feel better here, like a chef again. A victory at the Broiling Man Festival might be just the thing he needed to send him back home, ready to conquer the culinary world.

It wasn't just the aroma of gourmet coffee that wafted up the stairs to greet him. Julio was also frying up some amazing bacon, mesquite smoked if Neil was right, and his nose always was.

There were even some corn biscuits and flapjacks waiting, with smoked beans in syrup on the side.

"¡*Hola*, Neil!" Julio called as Neil made his way into the kitchen. Larry was already seated with two cups of coffee in front of him, chatting away with Feleena.

Neil took his seat and began heaping the food on his plate. Larry's eyes grew wide with wonder.

"Whoa!"

Neil wasn't usually a big eater—he was more of a taster and smeller—but he found himself with an unexpected appetite. The air, the joy of feeling better, and the incredible spread drove him on.

In a few minutes the entire plate was licked clean, and Neil leaned back in his chair with a satisfied sigh.

Larry beamed as he saw the smile play on Neil's lips. "What's next? You going to start drinking coffee?" Larry began to draw his mugs closer to his side of the table.

Neil shook his head. "No need. Señor Verde, that breakfast was invigorating."

"*Gracias*. Feleena deserves most of the credit. She takes care of our chickens and ducks, and that is why they lay such wonderful eggs."

"Lucky ducks," Larry said.

Feleena rolled her eyes. "So, onto the rules for the Broiling Man Festival," she said.

Neil leaned forward. "What do we need to know to get ready?"

"Rule number one. There are no rules. This is a celebration of cooking. Each chef is allowed to cook whatever they want, however they want."

Julio nodded. "We provide the main ingredients.

You can use anything we grow here on the farm, along with whatever you brought here, of course."

"From ribs and roasts to wheat and honey. If you can find it here, you can cook it here."

"No limits?" Neil said. He was already beginning to divide the various food smells he'd picked up at the ranch into possible combinations.

"Limits? This is the Wild West, pardner!" Feleena said, in her best cowgirl accent.

"Yee-haw!" Larry said. They stood up and hooked arms and began an impromptu hoedown in the kitchen.

Julio clapped and laughed.

Neil chuckled to himself. No limits? Chefs could cook whatever they wanted, however they wanted? This was going to be a cinch.

Feleena and Larry gave one final flourish and then sat down, laughing.

Julio clapped some more. "The festival starts tonight with the big bonfire. We Verdes cook this first night. After dinner is when Feleena will tell you the story of the map."

Feleena nodded. "But you have to work to earn the story, *and* your spot in the festival."

Neil raised an eyebrow. "What kind of work?" Angel had said this was a place to relax. Was Neil going to have to milk the cows?

Feleena rolled up her sleeves. "Honest work. We head to a part of the ranch that needs the brush cleared. It grows fast. We all clear a large area, then pitch in to dig the fire pit. The brush is burned the first night, and then we have the broiling pit that will be the site for all the cooking for the festival."

"Can I dress like a cowboy?" Larry said with a huge grin.

"Do they wear scuba gear?" Neil said.

"Ha-ha. I just want to rassle me some sagebrush and dig me a pit!" Larry said.

"How many other chefs are coming?" Neil asked, beginning to worry a bit about the idea of all that rasslin' and diggin' in the hot Arizona air.

Julio shrugged. "It depends. We are never certain until the first day."

As if on cue, a low rumbling began to shake the glassware on the table. Neil and Larry stood up and walked to the window over the tiled sink. A dust cloud appeared on the horizon. As it approached, Neil could see dozens of RVs and food trucks emerge.

"Many hands make light work," Larry said.

Neil nodded. *Many chefs make winning that much sweeter*, he thought.

CHAPTER FIVE

BROILING

Neil had never been so exhausted and, oddly, invigorated too. He, Larry, Feleena, Julio, and twenty other chefs had spent the day chopping down brush that seemed as thick as tree trunks. More chefs arrived as the day went on, dozens. Everyone chipped in, and they dug a huge pit in the middle of a far-flung field, dumped the brush inside, and set it on fire. Most of it was so dry it had gone up in flames like a giant baked Alaska.

Then they all sat down to an amazing meal of stew, more beans, and potatoes cooked in the hot coals. The stars came out one by one in the sky until it was almost filled.

Neil's face and hands were scratched and grimy.

But he was happy.

Why was he happy? Neil couldn't quite figure it out. Was it his impending and certain victory? It was certain, he could tell that instantly.

All the food trucks were parked alongside the FrankenWagon, in a circle around the fire pit. Close enough for Neil to get a good whiff of what they had to offer.

Neil looked at the other chefs, sitting around the glowing fire. He smirked. Walter Wheat and his Breaking Bread Bus? Amateur. He could smell the blue corn flour in Wheat's truck. Neil wouldn't feed that to cattle.

Jeri Garcia and her Kickin' Butte Montana Rib-Mobile? A hack. She was even using store-bought barbecue sauce mixed with some spices.

Erin-Marie Nade and her Vivacious Veggies Van? Close, but not close enough. The carrots she was storing were already turning from crisp to limp. Even rabbits wouldn't consider them gourmet.

Mary Maize didn't bother to bring any food or spices in her van. All Neil could smell were some almonds, but that was coming from her coat. Since she sat around eating granola trail mix all day, that wasn't a surprise.

Neil had this competition in the bag. He licked the remains of the baked beans off his spoon and stared into the fire, the flames dancing off his eyes.

"You look demented," Larry said, leaning toward him.

"Get your eyes checked. I'm just imagining the standing ovation I'm going to get when I give these amateurs a Neil Flambé dinner."

"I'm not sure you're fully entering into the spirit of this festival," Larry said. "I think these guys are a little more foodie than feud-ie, if you know what I mean."

Neil looked again at the circle of chefs. It was a hard crowd to pin down. They all seemed to be wearing weird outfits; tie-dyed shirts, skirts, hats, and even tie-dyed chef's jackets. Erin-Marie was dressed in a wool cap and faux-deerskin jacket. Barbara Brisket was wearing a jumpsuit she'd knitted herself from the remains of old oven mitts.

Some of the trucks were painted with psychedelic patterns, like one of Larry's tie-dyed me-shirts. Omar Poulet's Little Chicken food truck was powered by bicycles that the customers had to pedal if they wanted to get their order.

They were all somewhat crazier versions of Larry. No wonder Larry had been so stoked to . . . Neil stopped cold with a sudden realization. He turned his head and stared at Larry, who was smiling at him.

"This isn't a competition, is it?" Neil said.

Larry shook his head. "Sorry, cuz. I didn't want to break it to you when you were feeling so good. No duel. No cook-off. This is a big *celebration* of food. Everyone just kind of gets together for the week and . . . shares. No winners, no losers."

Neil watched as Larry reflexively lifted his hands to his ears, expecting a patented Neil Flambé explosion.

A short time before, maybe even a week before, news like this would have set Neil off. He would have gone on a rant about how he was better than anyone here. How the only thing he would share with these cooks was a lesson in how a real cook kicks butt.

Those thoughts were going through his brain now, but they were flickering out like sparks from the fire.

The stars twinkled. The fire burned. A coyote howled in the distance. The wind rustled the leaves of the trees. Neil could sense the physical presence of the nearby mountains, fields of grain, and even the animals. He looked around the circle again, at all the smiling faces, singing along as chef Stan Burns strummed his guitar, and he just couldn't believe in his anger anymore.

Assured victory wasn't what had made him feel so good. It was, he suspected, something more. Angel and Larry had kind of duped him, letting him think there was a competition at the end. He should care, but he didn't. But maybe they were right. Maybe being the best was fine without the need to prove it? Maybe?

Angel's last words before they'd left had been, "Go to the ranch. Go the festival. Find some inner peace."

Neil closed his eyes and listened. He threw the angry thoughts out of his head. Every part of him relaxed. He felt calm. He felt, possibly for the first time in his life, peace. Now that it was here, he could see that it had been coming over him in bits and pieces for months.

Neil thought of the empty trophy shelf in his room back home. Instead of blowing up, he shook his head and chuckled. He turned to Larry.

"No wonder you were so excited to be here. I get it."

Larry lowered his hands and gave Neil one of the biggest grins Neil had ever seen. "Welcome to the circle, chef boy," Larry said, slapping Neil on the shoulder. "Maybe you've turned a corner!"

"Maybe. Do circles have corners?"

Larry just laughed.

Neil wanted to call Isabella. He checked his phone. She'd still be at her convention. Instead he took a picture of the fire, with him and Larry smiling in front of it, and sent it to her.

Feeling the beauty, he wrote, blushing. It might be a little sappy, but it also expressed pretty closely what he was experiencing.

"Yeah, there's lots of beauty in Arizona," Larry said, reading over Neil's shoulder. He nodded his head at Feleena, who was wrapped in a blanket, singing along with some song about a cowboy and a tragic gunfight.

Neil rolled his eyes. "Just once I wish you'd focus on romaine over romance."

Larry's head shot back. "Your puns are even getting

almost funny! Angel was right. This place is miraculous."

"Ha-ha." Neil took a bit of brush from near his feet and threw it into the fire.

He caught Julio's eyes. Julio looked at Neil, smiled, and winked. Then Julio stood up and clapped his hands loudly. "I would like to welcome all of you to this year's Broiling Man Festival!"

There were whoops and cheers from the circle.

"For the next week we will all come together to cook, to celebrate food, to honor the earth and her bounty—to be or to become friends."

He punched the air, letting out a long loud cheer of "BROIL!"

"Broil, broil, broil!" everyone cheered.

Neil raised his arm in the air and let out a whoop. Then he laughed. He was surprising himself at every turn. This was all new territory.

Julio moved his hands up and down to calm everyone. "But we have a tradition to end this first night of the festival. For those of you who go back to the beginning, you will remember that my beloved wife would always end the bonfire with a story."

"The lost mine!" Burns yelled out, adding a huge whoop. He turned to Neil. "Love this story!"

Julio nodded solemnly. "My wife has joined the stars in the night sky. But the story lives on." He sat down. There was a moment of silence, and then Neil heard Feleena's voice, low and steady.

"I sat at this very fire, listening to her. I know the legend by heart, and with your permission I will continue the tradition."

Neil Flambé and the Duel in the Desert

Everyone nodded. Neil looked over at Feleena. She had moved closer to the fire, the red coals and dying embers illuminating her face.

"*Gracias.* Our story is a mystery. Some say it is a ghost story. It is the story of the lost gold mine of Guillermo Verde. "

As if on cue, the fire flickered higher.

Neil, like everyone else, was riveted.

Feleena began.

CHAPTER SIX

THE LEGEND
OF THE LOST
COOK'S MINE

The wilds of Arizona are littered with the bones of men and women who have tried to tame the land.

Still the people come, drawn by a voice heard in the depths of their souls that says, "This is a wild land, a dangerous land, but a free land where you can be anything you desire."

Many years ago the call reached the ears of a gentle young man named Guillermo Verde.

As the youngest of a large family, he knew he would inherit nothing. But his mother loved him and gave him her most precious gift, the ability to make the world a better place with wonderful food. After her death, Guillermo set out, with only her cast-iron skillet strapped on his back and her recipes scribbled in an old notebook.

He walked north from his home, braving the heat, the blazing sun, the coyote, the bandit, the scorpion, and the snake. Finally, at dawn on the twelfth day, he saw a town, blazing on the horizon.

Guillermo shuffled down the main street, his feet bare and bleeding, dust clinging to his every pore. Gunslingers and drunks, still awake from a night of debauchery, laughed at this scraggly-looking stranger. They fired bullets at the ground near his feet. Guillermo ignored them. He walked straight to the town's hotel and into the kitchen. In a daze, he set about cooking his mother's mole sauce.

He carefully melted the chocolate, ground the spices, and simmered the sauce, feeling the ghostly hand of his mother guiding his own, giving strength to his weakness. Guillermo stirred a final time, smelled the perfection of the dish, then fell to the ground. He surely would have died, but the owner of the hotel, drawn by the aroma, came through the door. He knew right away that Guillermo had created something amazing. One small taste confirmed it. Here, at the owner's feet, was that rare thing, a genius. He bent down and gave Guillermo a drink of water. Rather than call the sheriff, he hired Guillermo on the spot.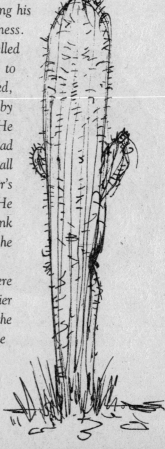

Soon Guillermo and the hotel were thriving. The legend grew of the frontier town with the magical chef. Even the roughest cowboy left feeling peaceable and calm after one of Guillermo's meals. Prospectors, after striking it rich, would drop down nuggets of pure gold, just to jump the line for dinner service. Peace reigned.

Guillermo, however, was not happy. Why not? He had fallen in love with the hotel waitress, Rosita, but was too shy to tell her.

One night, after the last diner had left, Rosita turned from locking the door to see a table, set for one with the hotel's finest china, lit by a lone candle. On the plate were lotus-flower sweets, wrapped in delicate pastry; cactus jellies served on wafer-thin slices of apple; tortillas handmade from the finest ground corn.

With each bite she felt her heart swell. By the time she had finished, she too was in love. She rushed to the kitchen and embraced Guillermo. A week later, they were married.

They used their savings to build a small cabin of wood and adobe, and that became their home. They were happy.

It was not to last.

Major Theodore Graves rode into town, accompanied by a dozen soldiers. He was known as "Gravestone" because of the men he had driven to their deaths through exhaustion or the bullet. It was debated whether he was hated more by his enemies or by his own troops. He used his authority to feed his own hunger for power and gold, for the very best of everything.

Gravestone stormed through the doors of the hotel kitchen, his pistol drawn.

"You will be my personal chef," Gravestone bellowed.

Guillermo didn't even look up from the dish he was preparing. "I cannot. My life is here."

"You come with me," Gravestone said, pointing his gun at Guillermo, "or you die."

Rosita burst into the room. "Leave him alone," she cried.

When Gravestone spied Rosita, his cruel soul twisted even more.

I came here to find a great chef, Gravestone thought. But I have also found a wife!

"You cannot take my husband," Rosita said.

Fire flashed behind Gravestone's eyes as his smirk turned to a scowl. Husband? Was there a way to have both the chef and Rosita? His mind raced.

Gravestone raised his gun and aimed at Rosita. He pulled back the hammer on his pistol but looked into Guillermo's eyes. "You come, or she will die."

Guillermo took Rosita's hand and pulled her close. "I must go," he whispered. "But I promise you I will return."

Gravestone holstered his gun but looked back at Rosita with an evil scowl as he and Guillermo walked out to the dusty street.

Rosita fell to her knees, weeping.

She would have wept more if she'd known Gravestone's true intentions. He was planning to steal Guillermo's recipes, then put a bullet into his back. Gravestone would make it look like Guillermo had been trying to escape. No one would mourn a coward, even his widow.

But a strange thing happened, a miracle, some say. As soon as the somber troop rode out of town, a giant storm hit—a storm of such ferocity and power that it hadn't been seen before or since. Perhaps it was Rosita's tears that sowed the skies.

For days the rain pounded down. Thick as a curtain it obscured the troop's vision and sent them marching in all directions. They were soon hopelessly lost.

The water rose and rose, refusing to sink into the hard soil. A flash flood swept the men and horses off their feet, sending them hurtling down a sudden and violent river. Gravestone's men clung to a wagon and floated away, never to be seen again.

Guillermo caught the roots of an ancient tree. He pulled himself to shore, then reached back and took Gravestone's hand. His mother's notebook slipped from within his shirt.

Gravestone lunged at it with

his free hand. Guillermo grabbed it first and stood up.

"I'll take it from your cold, dead hands," Gravestone hissed, reaching for his gun. As he let go of Guillermo, he began to fall back.

Guillermo turned and ran.

Gravestone, still half-immersed in water, fired.

As if moved by an unseen hand, Guillermo's skillet swung from his shoulder and deflected the shot.

Gravestone fired more shots even as he was carried away by the flood, but they all missed.

Guillermo ran faster and faster into the gloom, hoping to find shelter. A shaft of light broke through the clouds, the opening to a canyon. Guillermo spied a bat flying out from behind two boulders. A cave!

Guillermo slipped inside.

He watched from the shadows, worrying that Gravestone had escaped the waters and had followed him. Guillermo took a step back and fell.

He tumbled down for what seemed like forever and then landed with a thud. He expected to be immersed in darkness, but the walls shone like a sky filled with stars.

GOLD!

Guillermo filled his pockets, his hat, his boots. Then he began to look for a way out. He felt a breeze on his face and heard the sound of bats fluttering.

He followed the sound and the breeze through a maze of holes, cracks, and chasms and then finally felt the rush of fresh air. He breathed deeply and pushed through a tiny opening in the ground.

The rain had stopped.

He began walking home. Gravestone was nowhere to be seen or heard, but Guillermo kept to the shadows and walked in the cool of the night, just to be certain.

It took him a full seven days to reach the town. Rosita rushed out from the hotel, showering him with so many hugs and kisses that he feared his heart would burst with joy. He showed her the treasure and they talked excitedly about how they would buy all the land around their humble house, to make a ranch.

"But where is your mother's skillet?" Rosita asked.

Guillermo realized with sadness that he'd left the skillet behind in the cave. He had gold, yes, but had lost something precious.

"This is what comes from greed," he said.

"You can go back to get it," Rosita said.

Guillermo shook his head. "The lost skillet is a message. I took too much, more than I needed. We will buy our ranch, and we will never turn away a person in need."

Rosita nodded and hugged him even more tightly.

As for Gravestone, the river did not claim his life, but it changed him forever. He was thrown against canyon walls, tumbled by white-foamed rapids, and spat out onto the desert floor. Somewhere along the way he lost his pistol and then his mind. He emerged a broken man.

News reached him of Guillermo's miraculous find. He stole a horse and a shovel and spent the rest of his days wandering the wilderness in search of the chef's miraculous discovery.

He died mad, alone, and unloved. Although some still say they see his ghostly form searching, searching, searching.

Guillermo and Rosita died peacefully, minutes apart, at the ranch they'd founded, surrounded by their children and their children's children. Guillermo planted an olive tree each time one was born, and it's said the grove bowed down and wept the day he and Rosita died.

But that is not the end.

After they died, a map was discovered, hidden in the pages of Guillermo's recipe book. It showed the canyon where he took refuge from Gravestone, but precious few directions or markers.

And underneath the drawing of the canyon, there was a note that read:

I have staked a claim with the state. Whoever can present the skillet with the hole in the middle will be considered the rightful owner of the mine. My mother's name is inscribed on the handle. But only when a Verde is in real need and is of pure heart and great skill, will the mine be found again.

CHAPTER SEVEN

MINE ALL MINE

The fire had died down to glowing coals. Everyone was silent. Feleena fell back against her father's shoulder, exhausted.

"I love that story!" Walter said. "Makes me understand why this whole stretch of land is so special."

"Gives me the creeps every time I hear it," Erin-Marie said.

Feleena smiled. "It's really just a story about love." Then her smile turned into a long sigh. "There is much cooking tomorrow. Time for me to go get some sleep!" She stood up and brushed some loose bits of straw and weeds from her blanket. They fell on the coals, drying and cracking. The fire lit up Julio's face just enough for Neil to see tears in his eyes. Julio quickly dried the tears on his sleeve.

The other chefs rose and, nodding thanks to Julio and Feleena, went back to their trucks to sleep. Feleena kissed her father on the cheek and then walked off toward her horse, tied up a few yards away.

Julio still stared at the coals.

Neil sidled next to him. "I just wanted to say thanks again for having Larry and me here. It's been . . . wonderful."

Julio gave him a quick smile but continued to stare straight ahead. Neil saw that he was gripping his hands together so tightly that his knuckles were turning white.

"That map over the fireplace is the map from the story," Neil said.

Julio nodded. "*Sí*. That is the same map."

"Hasn't anyone been able to find the mine?"

"Many generations of Verdes have tried to break its code, but none have been successful. Some say there is a curse around the mine, set by Gravestone with his dying words. But that is a legend. Perhaps the time has not been right, or the need great enough."

Neil took a moment, thinking of what Julio had said about wishing the map were valuable. "You are in need right now, aren't you?"

Julio hung his head. "Yes. My wife's treatments were very expensive. The last few years, bad weather hurt our yield. Cattle have gone missing or been

46

killed by wild animals. It has been disaster after disaster. We appear on the surface to be doing well, but there is a wolf at the door." He threw some more brush into the fire and watched it burn.

"I have had to use the ranch as collateral for loans. I am paying them back, slowly. But now someone has come forward, offering to buy the land from the bank for much more than I owe. The bank looks only at the profit they can make, not what this place means to me and my family, and our guests."

"Who is the buyer?"

"I do not know. Someone rich. The bank says this person wants to turn the land into a subdivision of houses."

Neil shuddered.

A tear ran down Julio's cheek. "A miracle gold mine is exactly what we need, but it is, I am afraid, hopeless."

Neil was silent for a long time. He knew what it was like to keep a business afloat, and to watch it die. He'd just had that happen with Chez Flambé. But Salsa Verde was different. It was more than a business. It was, he felt, a *sacred* place. Neil looked at the circle of food trucks, felt the breeze, and heard the lone cry of a coyote in the distance. He thought of the amazing food that was grown here. The idea of all this being cut up and sold off to be turned into some development made him furious.

He stood up. "I'm going to find that mine," he said firmly. He caught Larry's eye. "*We* are going to help you save this place."

Larry stood up and let out a whoop. "Yeah! Team Flambé is back on the case!"

Julio smiled but shook his head. "The story is just a family legend. The map is real, but the chance of any real mine being out there is . . ." He shrugged and left it unsaid, but the suggestion was *zero*. "Time moves on. It was a dream to think that my family could keep this place going forever. A lovely dream, but we must all awaken sooner or later."

Neil took a deep breath. He had solved numerous mysteries. Something, a sense, a tingling in his fingers, told him that there was an actual gold mine out there. This Guillermo Verde had been a chef, by all accounts a great chef. There would be clues, signs, something left for a future chef to follow. Neil had cracked tougher cases than this. Besides, this time there was no real danger or threat, just a cold trail, left by a great chef, for another great chef to follow.

"I think it's more than a legend. Señor Verde, we are going to find that mine and we are going to start now."

Julio stood up and shook Neil's hand. "Well, I cannot but thank you. But I ask one small favor."

"Yes?"

"That you stay here for one more day, to cook for the other chefs. This festival means so much to my daughter and me, and the thought of you leaving before we can experience your wonderful broiling techniques . . . it is a sad thought. The mine can stay hidden for one more day. Stay and refresh yourself with our friends, and then you will be fully prepared for your journey."

Neil considered, and nodded. "Agreed."

Larry added a loud "Yee-HAW!"

CHAPTER EIGHT

ROAM ON THE RANGE

Two days later Neil and Larry packed up the FrankenWagon and got ready to head out. Neil's whole smoked chicken and grilled veggies had been, as expected, a huge hit.

The other chefs lined up around the fire pit to see them off.

"Hey! Good luck, daddyo," said a chef named Zach Keeney. Then he went back to knitting the napkins for his dinner that night.

Mary Maize, strumming what looked like a

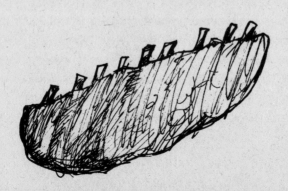

homemade guitar that was held together by old rubber bands, waved at them. "Someone sets out almost every festival after hearing that story." She still smelled like almonds, Neil noticed.

Walter nodded. "Me and a couple of the other cooks tried a few years ago."

"Did you find anything?" Neil asked.

"Easier said than done," Erin-Marie added. "We took pictures of the map and everything, but still couldn't figure out where it was telling us to look."

Mary nodded. "It shows a valley or canyon, sort of like this one. But the problem is it looks like almost every valley in the state, and not perfectly like any of them."

Neil was starting to feel his determination weaken. Then he remembered that none of these others had his nose, his knowledge of cooking, and his experience as a detective. He'd succeed where others had fallen short. That was what he always did.

"I appreciate the advice," he said.

"And it's not like the Verdes are really in need," Mary said, taking in the whole vista with a wave of her hand.

Neil didn't feel it was fair to share the news that the ranch was in some serious financial trouble, so he kept that to himself. "Well, good luck. And Larry said this was a festival for sharing, so I've got a present for you all."

Neil opened a cardboard box. Inside were ten bottles of his very own barbecue sauce.

The other chefs oohed and aahed.

But he wasn't done. Neil handed Walter Wheat his recipe for spitfire ribs with a dry spice rub. It was one of his go-to grill dishes at Chez Flambé. Neil had never even shared the spice combination with Larry. "It's really good, and will go really well with your corn bread… if you pull back on the salted butter just a touch."

Walter held the recipe like a precious Fabergé egg. "Whoa, thanks! Now go find that treasure fast and then get back here!"

Neil smiled, then went around the pit shaking everyone's hands. He hoped they found the mine fast. He wanted to come back to this wonderful place.

Larry's eyes grew wide as he watched Neil, but he said nothing. He just shook his head and smiled as Neil walked past him and into the FrankenWagon.

"What?" Neil said, looking at the weird expression on Larry's face.

"Who are you, really? And what have you done to my obnoxious cousin?"

"I'm not sure myself," Neil said, running his hand through his hair. "But I do know that this place needs to be saved, and we are the ones to do it."

Larry took his seat and fired up the engine.

He reached over to give Neil a high five. Neil flinched.

"Okay. Still some work to do on your loosening up," Larry said.

"I was flinching because your armpit smells like three-week-old rotten milk."

Larry raised his arm and took a whiff. "Good point. Let's head to the ranch house and get the map."

"And take a shower."

"Dealio!"

CHAPTER NINE

TRACKS

Larry turned on the engine of the FrankenWagon, waved good-bye to the Verdes, and drove away. He gave a deep sigh. As they passed the rows of olive trees, Neil thought of all the grandchildren Guillermo and Rosita had celebrated. There had to be a hundred trees. They smelled amazing.

"Too bad Feleena couldn't join us," Larry said.

Neil watched the trees recede in the distance. "Maybe you should have told her about the scuba gear."

"She would have gone for it. She's cool."

"Anyway, she said to call her if we make any progress," Neil said.

"So where are we heading?" Larry asked as they drove up the slope.

"The site of the original town is a few miles away. Seems as good a place to start as any."

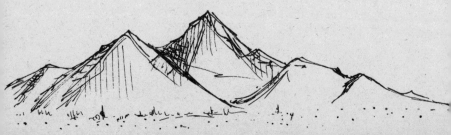

"It's close, so it's got that going for it."

"It's called Pick-Me-Up. Even Feleena didn't know why."

"Maybe it's home to a lot of coffee shops!" Larry said hopefully. He swigged the last molecule from his morning coffee. "I need a pick-me-up!"

"Good luck. Feleena said it's a ghost town now," Neil said.

Larry sagged in the driver's seat. "How far away is this desolate coffee-free wasteland?"

"About a twenty-minute drive."

"I'll stop and brew some more java before we go exploring. Hey, even the thought really perks me up! Get it? Perks?"

"Hmmmm," Neil said, distracted. He'd turned his attention from Larry's caffeine puns to Guillermo's treasure map. He reached into the glove compartment and pulled out a cookbook. Tucked inside, in a heavy-duty plastic freezer bag, was the original.

The map was quite small, about the size of a square dessert plate. There were precious few details. Guillermo had drawn a valley, jagged and deep. There was a large X next to two oval boulders. Larry thought they looked like eggs. Both agreed they marked the hidden entrance to the mine.

Nearby was a crudely drawn bunch of cactus. Neil thought they looked more like broccoli.

"Eggs and broccoli. That Guillermo liked his food," Larry said.

To the right of the valley was a drawing of some kind of pueblo dwelling, carved into the side of a hill.

Neil looked from the map to the surrounding countryside to see if anything matched the canyon on the map. Nothing.

He looked at a map of Arizona that he'd downloaded onto his phone. "There are hundreds of valleys and canyons."

"But that close to a bunch of cacti and a pueblo dwelling? That must narrow things down a lot."

Neil did a quick search on his phone. "There are lots of pueblo dwellings all over the state. And I don't know if you've noticed, but cacti are not rare. So, not really. There must be some other clue in the map."

"Seems like someone would have used a satellite image to find it by now."

Neil nodded. "Or maybe the map is wrong, or he was just dazed, or sick when he made it. It's not exactly a detailed masterpiece."

"Any, you know, *aromatic* clues?" Larry asked.

"I'll check again." Neil carefully lifted the plastic up by one corner.

There was a reason Neil had asked Julio for the original.

Neil knew from experience that there might still be clues hidden in the paper; smells that might help give him a scent to follow. The same sorts of tiny clues, everything from traces of ancient lemon and honey to traces of tea, had proven crucial in numerous other cases.

Neil gently raised the exposed map to his nose. He couldn't smell anything other than the aroma of old paper, some very faint processed spices, probably residue from being so close to the modern kitchen of Salsa Verde, and the metallic remains of mineral dust. That was everywhere and on everything in this dusty, windy state.

The mystery wasn't going to be cracked so easily. Neil frowned and placed the map back in the cookbook.

"I think that's the town just ahead," Larry said, pointing. "Or what's left of it."

A dusty pile of rubble came into view. Larry pulled onto what was once the main road, the very road Guillermo had walked down more than a century before, although it was hard for Neil to imagine.

Larry had to swerve to avoid the cacti that had grown in the middle of what used to be the road. Brush and weeds filled up almost every other space, at least the parts that weren't rock, sand, or animal bones. Planks of wood, scorched gray by the sun, the grains open wide from the lack of moisture, lay strewn and piled all over the ground.

Larry turned off the FrankenWagon, and he and Neil climbed down from the cabin.

Larry shook his head. "Ghost town? I bet even a ghost would stay away from this place."

"Julio said the town was still inhabited even a few decades ago. It's amazing how fast the desert can just swallow it up."

Larry pointed to a low wall of wind-blasted stones. "That looks like the foundation of a pretty big building. I'll bet that's what's left of the hotel."

They walked over and stared into the large stone-lined pit. "The basement," Neil said, kneeling down at the edge. He picked up a piece of rock, smelled it, and then threw it onto the dirt, sand, wood, and brick that had practically filled up the hole.

"Well, this is underwhelming," Larry said.

Neil stood up. "Agreed. But we might as well look around for a bit."

They began to sift through some of the loose planks, walking around and trying to re-create what this town might have been like when Guillermo, Rosita, and Gravestone had walked the earth.

To keep himself entertained, Larry started strutting as if he were a cowboy getting ready for a duel. He spread his legs wide, with long, exaggerated steps. "The Wild West! It must have been so cool to just saunter into town, get off'n yer horse, and stare down a gunslinger like Gravestone."

Neil ignored him and closed his eyes, smelling the air. He kept hoping he'd pick up something out of the ordinary, or sense something that only a chef would recognize as a clue. But it was hopeless.

Larry slipped into an even thicker cowboy drawl. "Gravestone, prepare to meet yer maker. This town ain't big enough for the two of us."

"There are three of us," Neil said.

Larry continued. "Pay no attention to my sidekick, Slappy Neil. He's just here for comic relief."

"Slappy?"

"Now, Gravestone. Where is the lost mine of El Guillermo Verde? Speak! At least when I shoot ya, you can die with a clean conscience."

"That is the worst accent I've ever heard," Neil said. He went back to sniffing the air.

Larry ignored him. "I know what I'm missing! Spurs." He began making a sound effect with every step. "Clink, clink, clink," he said, continuing to march forward.

Neil wiped sweat from his forehead. "I think your ratty sneakers and me-shirt are kind of killing the day-dream."

Larry looked at his shoes. "That's part of the plan, pardner. While that no-good varmint is gawking at my fancy city-slicker clothes, I'll surprise him and draw first!"

"You can barely draw a stick figure."

"Ha-ha." Larry pointed his finger and started making noises like an old western gunfight. "Pow! Pow!" Then he blew on the tip of his finger and stuck it back in an imaginary holster. "Anyway, Slappy, there ain't nuthin' hereabouts worth looking at. I'm going to make some coffee."

Larry "clinked" off to the FrankenWagon, while Neil continued to walk around the town. He wasn't really expecting to find anything anymore. But he liked the fact that he was in a place where Guillermo had been a great chef. Guillermo's story had him thinking. Guillermo had started a new life here. It hadn't been a ghost town then, but it had definitely been small and remote.

Neil thought of his own uncertain future. Maybe he'd need to move far away from home to start over. Maybe he could start everything fresh, find a desperate town with a hotel in need of a super-chef to turn it from backwater to brilliant.

Of course, his parents would make him graduate high school first. "Ugh," he said as his dream evaporated like a mirage.

Larry was right. There was nothing to see here. It was time to move on.

According to Feleena's story, Gravestone and Guillermo had marched for days after the storms had come up.

The map didn't really suggest which direction they'd headed. A few days in either direction could take them almost anywhere. He started walking back to the FrankenWagon.

"All right, Lasso Larry, let's hitch up the pony and leave Pick-Me-Up. I guess our best bet is . . ." He stopped.

A very slight breeze came up. It carried a new smell, bat guano. No, not bat guano precisely, but something similar.

He hadn't seen any sign of bats flying around. The smell was tweaking something.

"Bat guano, bat guano, bat guano," he said to himself. It clicked.

Larry had been read-
ing up on the Old West for
their trip and had delighted in
throwing gross facts Neil's way.

Bat guano was used in the
Old West to make saltpeter. And
saltpeter, Larry had pointed out,
was one of the main ingredients of
gunpowder.

Neil sniffed again. It was incredibly faint, but he
could smell, along with the guano, traces of sulfur and
charred wood. Now he was sure of it. He was smelling
some old style of gunpowder.

Neil looked around. Everything looked exactly the
same. Nothing but cacti and ruins. He couldn't see anything new in the surrounding countryside.

Was this place haunted?

Was he imagining things?

He stood up and cocked an ear. All he could hear
was the rustle of the wind on the grasses and brush. But
the smell was still there. Faint, but unmistakable.

Neil slapped the dust off his knees and walked
quickly, but not too quickly, back to the FrankenWagon.

"I think we should get moving," he said quietly as he
climbed into his seat.

"In a second," Larry said, his feet propped on the
dashboard, a mug of coffee in his hands.

"I don't think we're alone," Neil said, trying to look
calm. "And whoever is out there has a gun."

Larry's eyes grew wide. "The super-nose is never
wrong."

He lowered his legs slowly and turned the ignition key. "I guess there's nothing here," he said loud enough to be heard through his open window. "Let's get a move on, pardner."

Larry gunned the engine, turned around, and bombed back down the road the way they'd come. No one who'd ever seen Larry drive would be suspicious.

"Which way was the wind coming from?"

"This way," Neil said, pointing straight ahead.

"Wait, so we're heading *toward* the dude with the gun?"

"Maybe it's not a person. Maybe it's some old arms depot in the ghost town that's buried under the rubble."

"Uh-huh. Was the smell there the whole time?"

"I don't think so. It showed up while I was looking around."

"Like I said, a dude with a gun." Larry slammed on the brakes and turned off the engine. "Maybe have another sniff." He opened his door and jumped out.

"Good idea," Neil said. "Pretend you need a pee break and look around."

"Um, yeah. Pretend," Larry said, rushing over to the tall grass.

Neil opened his window and sniffed the air.

The smell was gone. That meant they'd either passed the source, or Larry had scared off whoever or whatever it was with his crazy driving.

Or maybe, Neil thought with a shudder, it was a ghost.

CHAPTER TEN

ON THE ROAD . . . AGAIN

G hosts don't need guns," Larry said. "And they probably don't smell like gunpowder."

"I didn't say it was a ghost. It's just, I don't know, that story Feleena told us, and the idea that Gravestone just kind of disappeared into the mountains . . . all that just gives me the creeps."

Larry looked at Neil and grinned. "You really didn't spend a lot of time at summer camp, did you?"

"You know I didn't," Neil said. He had actually gone to summer camp, once, when Larry had been a counselor. It had not gone well. Neil had stood on a table during the very first meal and accused the cook of trying to kill everyone with tinned beef rations from the Stone Age. The campers had chosen sides, and the ensuing food fight was still talked about in hushed tones around the campfires.

"That's how you tell a good campfire story, that's all. Remember the curse on our family?"

Neil shuddered again but nodded. "I know, not a real curse."

"There was no magic there, just a lot of nutjob chefs who wanted all the Flambés wiped out. So don't sweat the supernatural stuff. I mean, even if a ghost had a gun, it would probably shoot ghost bullets. They'd go through you faster than . . . ?"

Neil smiled. He knew Larry's games. "Than fast-food poutine."

"With about the same nutritional value, too. I was going to say, a laxative shake."

Neil laughed. Larry always had a gift for lightening up even the most serious situations.

"How about a warm prune smoothie?"

Larry guffawed loudly. "All right, you win. That's disgusting."

"Thank you."

"So, where are we heading, chef boy? Any magical advice yet? We're almost back at the main highway."

Neil held the original map in his lap again, hoping that it would show them which way to drive, like a divining rod for treasure. He held it up to the window and saw something he hadn't noticed before. There was writing on the other side.

He flipped the paper over. His heart gave a leap. "It's a recipe from Guillermo's recipe book!"

"Feleena said it was from the recipe book."

"But she didn't say it was written *in* the book. I just assumed it had been tucked inside. I didn't even think to look." He smacked his head with his palm.

Larry took his eyes off the road for a second to take a look. "What does it say?"

Neil scanned the notes and amounts. "It looks like a recipe for batter."

"Batter? Like cake batter?"

"Yes," Neil said.

Larry beamed. "Hey! Maybe it's a special kind of batter? Like 'the gold mine is here' batter?"

Neil turned the paper back and forth and even held it up to the midday sun to see if there were any extra markings. "No. Just a recipe for a really basic cake batter. Only five ingredients—butter, eggs, milk, flour, and sugar—and a note saying, 'Top with fruits.'"

"Fruits?"

"Fruits."

"If that's a code, it's not an obvious one! Anyway, someone must have tried to link the recipe to the mine before."

Neil thought for a moment. "Not the other cooks at the festival. They were only going by photos of the front of the page, the part with the map. So, really, nobody has seen this other side since Julio was a boy, when that fire happened."

"It's been in that frame ever since."

Neil nodded. "Still, not something to dismiss." He began tapping his finger against his upper lip, thinking. "Cake, cake . . ."

"Keep it in the back of your brain oven, cuz. Stuff has a way of cooking on its own back there."

"Thanks."

"Except your biology homework." Larry chuckled.

"Ha-ha. Anyway, I'm going to say we head north. Only because there are more canyons and valleys that way."

"You do know how big a state this is, right?"

"Something will click, I hope."

"I have faith in you," Larry said. He turned onto the highway and headed north.

Neil was starting to realize what a stupid idea it had been to just head out without a plan. "Like finding a needle in a haystack," he said, watching more and more desert and brush roll past his window.

"That's good news!" Larry said.

"How do you figure?"

"This state is ninety percent desert. How many haystacks can there possibly be?"

Neil put the map away. He pulled out his phone and looked at the satellite image of the state. Arizona seemed to have been gouged by rivers, tornadoes, and floods, and it had valleys and canyons all over the place, but none that seemed to fit all the other criteria. He narrowed his search to everything within a week's hike of Salsa Verde and Pick-Me-Up, which didn't really narrow things down much at all.

His phone pinged.

"What's that?" Larry asked.

"A text from Isabella. 'Just getting on plane. Long flight with no service. Details later. Have a great trip.'"

"Plane?"

"Yeah, I didn't know she was flying anywhere else," Neil said.

"Maybe she landed some big contract at the convention."

Neil nodded. He texted back, *Safe flight. Will update you on progress here. Still having a good time.*

Isabella didn't respond.

"While we're driving, let's play another game," Larry said.

"Fine. What?"

"City search. We'll see how fast you can find the weirdest town name in Arizona on the map. Then we'll see how many we can find."

"How many could there be?"

"Hundreds! Feleena and I were talking last night, and she was saying that Arizona is riddled with them, 'like bullet holes through a horse thief!'"

"Weirder than Pick-Me-Up?"

"Are you kidding? That's the vanilla of weird place names!"

Neil frowned. "I've never understood why vanilla gets such a bad name. When I cook with vanilla, it blows your mind."

"It's just a figure of speech."

"It's a stupid figure of speech."

"Fine. Pick-Me-Up is the processed white bread of weird place names."

"Better. Although I could still blow your mind with white bread."

Larry gave a sarcastic cough. "Fine, you're the greatest. Now, find Obnoxious Chef on the map."

Neil began poring over the map on his phone but stopped when he heard Larry snickering.

"That wasn't funny." But he grinned, watching Larry enjoy himself so much. "Okay, give me a real one."

"Why."

"Because I asked you to."

"I know. Why."

Neil narrowed his eyes and stared at Larry. "Because. I. Asked. You. To. This is your stupid game."

"Why."

"I DON'T KNOW WHY!!!!" Neil yelled.

Larry beamed. "I know. That's why I asked you to find it on the map. So far, it's taken you ten seconds."

"You are seriously saying that there's a Why, Arizona?"

Larry nodded. "Eleven. Twelve. Thirteen."

"FINE! I'm looking!" Neil began to scan the map. A minute or so later he found it: Why, Arizona, tucked into the bottom left of the state.

"Cool! I got it! Give me another. And don't say Why again."

Larry rubbed his chin. "Okay."

Neil began searching the map.

"There's no Okay, okay? I was just thinking out loud. Okay, Feleena mentioned one called Total Wreck. There's even a nice story I can tell you if you find it in thirty seconds! Go!"

Neil scrambled to the map. It took more than thirty seconds, but Total Wreck finally jumped out, in the bottom right corner of the state. "Got it," Neil said. "So is the story about the name?"

Larry shook his head. "No. So the story is that a local guy there got into a gunfight once. He was shot, but the bullet didn't kill him. It was stopped by a pack of love letters the man had stuffed in his chest pocket. He later married the girl who'd written the letters."

Neil grinned.

"What's so funny?"

"Nothing," Neil said, blushing.

"Wait. Don't tell me Isabella gave you some letters before we left!" Larry was practically jumping up and down in his seat. "Nice to see you've got some of the Larry charisma after all!"

Neil patted his chest. "Isabella gave me three letters. She said I should open one a week until I get back home."

"I can imagine. Letter one. 'Dear Neil, how I miss you. XXXOOO. Kissy kissy.' Letter three. 'Dear Nate. Forgetting what you look like.'"

Neil reached across and punched Larry in the

shoulder. "Ha-ha. All right, give me another name."

"Strawberry."

"You're making that up."

Larry shook his head. "Nope."

Neil began to look for Strawberry, then stopped. "Wait a minute. The map Guillermo left. On the back it says, 'Top with fruits.' Maybe that's the cheffy clue I've been looking for!"

Larry nodded. "Makes some sense."

"It's exactly the kind of clue a chef would leave for a chef to find."

"Back on the case!"

"I *knew* there'd be a food connection."

Larry beamed. "Worth a shot, pardner. Where is it?"

Neil typed in a search for Strawberry, Arizona. He smiled. "We're on the way there! It's not too far. A few hours straight ahead."

"Let's see if it has a valley nearby!" Larry gunned the engine and they were off.

"And some pueblo dwellings!"

"And a coffee shop!"

CHAPTER ELEVEN

STRAWBERRY SHORTCUT?

Unlike Pick-Me-Up, Strawberry still had buildings and stores, and people. People who stared in shock as Larry sped the FrankenWagon down the main street and screeched to a stop.

The town was situated in the center of the state. It was up in the hills, surrounded by tall pine trees. Neil rolled down his window and smelled the fresh air, relaxing slowly and fighting a slight case of Larry-driving-induced nausea. The trip had been bumpy. Reading the guidebook to rural Arizona towns while Larry gunned around treacherous turns hadn't helped.

"So, chef boy, what are we looking for? You think Guillermo was saying the mine is here in Strawberry?"

"Let's say he was here, a century ago. Maybe the people here can tell us if there's a valley nearby that looks like the one on the map."

"That's one idea."

Another thought occurred to Neil. "Or maybe

Guillermo came through here himself on the journey home and left some clues behind that we're supposed to follow."

"Just like our last case. The map is a map not to the treasure, but to the clues you need to help find the treasure."

"The town is old enough. It was here when Gravestone and Guillermo were wandering the desert." Neil pointed at a sign by the road. It stood in front of an old log house. The sign said STRAWBERRY SCHOOLHOUSE—THE OLDEST STANDING SCHOOL IN ARIZONA.

"Those kids must have gotten tired!" Larry joked. "I wonder where the oldest sitting school was?"

"Ha, ha, ha. The point is that the schoolhouse is from the 1800s. Maybe there's something inside that's a clue."

"Maybe he carved something in the wood, like a trail marker?"

Neil nodded. "Think of how often we end up with a tiny part of a puzzle, but we can use that to piece the larger picture together."

"Like reconstructing a recipe from just one ingredient."

"Yeah. But right now we don't have a piece yet."

"Let's get started!" Larry hopped down from the cab and waved at a passing woman. "Howdy, ma'am, can I ask you a question?"

The woman scurried away without answering.

Larry tried calling out to some other men and women, but they ducked their heads and walked by briskly.

"Friendly town," Larry said.

Neil watched as person after person stole a glance at the FrankenWagon and then quickened their pace. "I think the problem might be us."

Larry looked shocked. "You think they're scared by Frankie?"

"Frankie? I think so, yes."

"They have no taste."

"Taste, taste," Neil said. "Good idea."

"Um, thanks?"

"It's almost dinnertime. I have an idea to win them over. Let's cook."

Larry smiled. "And then they'll come to us. The brain is catching up to the super-nose! Man, this trip is really turning you into the new Neil."

Neil smiled and walked into the wagon. They'd left much of their luggage back at the ranch, so the workstation was actually pretty clear. He fired up the ovens and the stove and began prepping some dinner.

Larry took out a sandwich board and wrote down the menu.

They had worked out a series of food-truck-style foods—tacos, mini-burgers, sausages—foods you could eat as you stood, chatted, or even continued on your way to work. It wasn't Neil's preferred environment, but once they'd decided on the food truck, Neil had vowed to master that world as well.

The cramped quarters heated up quickly, but Neil

felt happy as the food began to turn from raw potential to cooked perfection. He was enjoying himself more than he expected.

Larry came inside and opened the service window. The window locked open, and Larry hooked a large stainless-steel serving tray in the opening. He quickly covered it with a series of dips, sauces, condiments, and cutlery and then hung a bell on the side.

Soon the smells of the cooking wafted over the town. Like the music of the Pied Piper, the aroma of Neil's cooking drew people toward the van.

A man approached, sniffing the air tentatively but with a growing smile. He rang the bell. Larry stuck his head out and said in an incredibly high-pitched shriek, "Who rang that bell?"

The man looked confused and took a step back.

"Sorry, man, couldn't resist. It's from *The Wizard of Oz*. The gatekeeper guy yells that at Dorothy, remember? He's got that awesome furry hat on?"

"Oh . . . um, isn't this a food truck?"

Neil could tell Larry was about to say something else goofy, so he raised a spatula and held it near Larry's rear end.

"A food truck? Well, yes and no. It's actually a magical mystery—OUCH!!!!! HEY! I mean, yes, yes it is"—Larry reached back and rubbed his butt—"a food truck."

"It smells amazing. I'll take two of those fish tacos and maybe some of those oven-roasted potatoes."

"Coming right up!" Larry said, and he called back to Neil, "Two Gill Hodges and a side of Flaming Murphys."

"What?" Neil said.

"I made a list of deli slang. It's tacked up over the sink."

Neil looked at the list.

Eggs were "Chicken Bombs."

Burgers were "Hockey Pucks."

Fish tacos were "Gill Hodges."

"Gill Hodges?"

"Old-time baseball player. I've always wanted to talk like a waitress, ever since we met Dinah Saucer."

"Who?"

"The cool waitress at that diner we hit in Penticton a couple of months back?"

Neil vaguely remembered the diner. It had smelled of grease and burned eggs.

"Wait, didn't Dinah pour coffee on my head?"

Larry nodded. "You'd told her leaving a tip would only encourage the restaurant to poison more customers."

"She wasn't even the cook!" Neil said. "And I was right. Those eggs were rancid."

"Dinah called them Chicken Bombs with a Side of Ham Slams. She was a real poet."

"Could she make up a rhyme for botulism?" Neil said under his breath.

"Got You Prism," Larry said.

Neil rolled his eyes and went back to cooking.

A crowd had gathered outside, and Neil heard them actually *ooh* as Larry passed through the first succulent plate of food.

"Looks great! How much?" the man asked.

"Free!"

"Free? Wow! Thanks."

"Free?" Neil nearly choked. He grabbed the spatula and took another swipe at Larry. The spatula made a metallic sound and vibrated in Neil's hand so much he dropped it, a pain shooting up his forearm. Larry turned, grinned, and pulled a pie tin from inside his jeans. Then he put it back in, winked, and turned back to the customer.

"Well, *almost* free. We have a few questions. In return for some answers, we offer a whole menu of delectable delights."

There was a flurry of called-out orders as the townsfolk rushed to get in on the deal.

As Neil furiously cooked, he heard snippets of the conversation coming back through the sliding service window of the FrankenWagon.

Yes, other chefs in food trucks had come through here. Now that Larry asked, yes, some of them had said they were looking for a lost gold mine. The locals thought that was weird and had sent them on their way.

"There's no gold mine near here that has anything left in it but rock."

Yes, there were still buildings here that would have been around a century ago: the schoolhouse and some old buildings from when the town was a center for mining.

"They're closed for the day, but if you throw in some yam fries, I'll let you in tomorrow."

Neil threw the hand-cut yams into the sizzling deep fryer.

Pueblo dwellings? Not close by, but certainly there were many near Flagstaff, further north.

Neil frowned as he heard that news.

No, there were no stands of tall broccoli or trees that looked like broccoli. "Just lots and lots of pine."

Three hours later everyone had been fed, and every question had been answered.

Neil and Larry cleaned up and then sat in the cab of the FrankenWagon to compare notes from the first day of their treasure hunt.

"We'd better find this mine soon," Neil said, "or we're going to be as broke as the Verdes."

"I've factored it all into the finder's fee," Larry said, sipping his coffee. He pulled a lever near his feet and tilted his seat back until it was almost parallel with the floor. He gave a satisfied sigh and plopped his feet on the steering wheel.

"I'm so glad I replaced the old seats with these recliners I found in the dump."

"That explains the smell," Neil said.

"Next time I'm putting in hammocks! Imagine me driving while swaying back and forth."

"I'm not sure that's a good idea, or legal."

"Thanks for the buzzkill, Dad," Larry said. "Now, as I see it, the buildings here are probably worth a look."

"I think I heard them mention there was free fair-trade coffee waiting for you at the schoolhouse museum tomorrow."

Larry feigned surprise. "Really?! What an unexpected bonus!"

Neil frowned. "I wish we weren't just following those

other chefs. They've probably already followed all these leads."

"Team Flambé is smarter than all those other chefs put together. They were just looking for any town named after food. But we have experience, your superior cheffy instincts, and my detective brain."

"Did you say 'defective'?"

"Very funny. Even if we follow the same ground, we have some major advantages over the others. We've done this map-and-code thing before."

"True. And if we don't find anything in the buildings, I guess we head outside the town and look around for that stupid valley."

"Flagstaff sounds promising. It's not a kind of fruit too, is it?"

"No." Neil sat and thought for a bit as Larry sipped his coffee. "I hope Strawberry wasn't a dead end."

"We'll see tomorrow."

A cool breeze came in through Neil's window, and he shivered. "It does get cold here at night," he said, reaching for the handle.

He stopped. On the wind, again, came the faint aroma of saltpeter. It was only there for a second and then it disappeared. He looked around as he slowly rolled up his window. The streetlights and house lamps gave the shadows a kind of eerie shimmer, but he couldn't see anything moving other than a few birds and tree branches.

The wind hadn't changed direction, but the smell was gone. He closed his window and wrapped himself in a blanket. He was still shivering now, but not because of the cold.

"All good, cuz?"

"I think I should turn in. I'm imagining things," Neil said. And as soon as he said it, he felt an overwhelming fatigue. It had been a long day.

Larry flicked off the lamp. "Sleep. Good idea." Within moments he was snoring away, his coffee mug rising and falling gently on his stomach. How could Larry sleep like that? Neil wondered.

Neil walked back to his bed, an old yoga mat that he'd tucked under the sink. He pulled it out and then laid some blankets on top.

He crawled in and took a deep breath. The lingering smells of dinner enveloped him like a soft duvet. Neil had never had a teddy bear. He had snuggled with a spatula for a while. He didn't need anything like that anymore, but he had to admit that it was soothing and comforting to fall asleep surrounded by all his cooking equipment.

As he rested his head on his pillow, his mind drifted back to the recipe on the back of the map. Neil had been so sure that Strawberry, Arizona, had been the starting point for resolving this mystery. But they hadn't even been the first ones to think of connecting food to the search for the mine. Of course, those chefs had been taking a stab in the dark with a dull blade. Neil had seen the actual recipe.

Neil ran it through his head again. Cover with fruits, it had said. What kind of fruit? Wait . . . not fruit but fruits. FruitS!

Neil sat up straight.

The recipe hadn't said fruit, it had said fruits, plural. The word "fruit" could be both plural or singular, so why add the *s*?

Neil jumped out of bed and ran up to the cab. He shook Larry awake.

Larry instinctively took a swig from his mug. His eyes popped open. "Whoa, coffee's still warm. I guess I wasn't out long. What's up?"

"Fruits."

"Finally admitting you're bananas?"

"No, no. Guillermo didn't say that you covered the cake with fruit. He said *fruits*. Are there any other places named for fruits?"

Larry swigged his coffee again. "Let's *seed* what we can find." He pulled out his phone and did a quick search. "Well, it's our lucky day. There's a place near the Grand Canyon called Peach Springs." He held up his phone.

"I knew it!" Neil said. "I'll bet the mine is somewhere between here and there. We just have to connect the dots."

"It's a good theory."

Neil smiled. "The pueblo stuff and the trees should be close by."

"So, should we head out right away?"

Neil thought of the ghostly gunpowder smell and considered bolting right away. But that was absurd. "No, we should still hit the schoolhouse just to be sure."

Larry slid back down in his chair and clicked

off his phone. "Now this is starting to feel more like a real Team Flambé mystery!"

"If we don't see the valley on the way, I guess we can hike around the Grand Canyon for a bit and see if it's there."

Larry laughed. "Yeah, we should be able to get from side to side in minutes."

"Why, how big can it be?"

"You're joking, right?"

Neil shrugged. "It's called Grand, not Gigantic."

Larry chuckled. "And you call *me* an idiot."

CHAPTER TWELVE

GRAND

Neil had seen pictures of the Grand Canyon. He'd heard people, even his workaholic parents, describe how unexpectedly awesome the place could be, but he had assumed it wouldn't live up to the billing. So little did, in his few years of experience, outside of his own cooking.

But the Grand Canyon was better, and bigger, than any idea Neil had been able to conjure in his imagination. Summits and rock plateaus in vibrant rose, red orange, and pink stood like so many perfect peaks of meringue as far as the eye could see. There were traces of a recent snowfall clinging to the south side of the formations, looking almost electric blue in the shadows of the red stones. A band of silver glinted in the early morning light, impossibly far below in the canyon floor.

For the first time since they'd left home, even Larry was speechless, for a few minutes anyway.

Neil sat down on a ledge and stared. It was like a physical embodiment of the peace he'd been feeling inside ever since he'd arrived in Arizona. It gave him an

even stronger desire to help find the mine, to keep the Verdes' ranch from closing down.

"A lot of the rock formations are named after spiritual temples," Larry said, sitting down next to Neil.

"I can see why."

"Of course, there's also a Devil's Corkscrew."

Neil didn't move, even to shrug. "Even that doesn't ruin the moment."

After a few minutes of silence Neil took his phone, snapped a picture, and sent it to Isabella.

"You also notice, chef boy, that there are a lot of valleys," Larry said.

"I guess that stream could be the river from the legend. A good rainfall would certainly make it bigger."

"That river is huge. It only looks small because we're so far above it. It was actually that river that carved all of this." Larry spread his hands wide to take in as much of the expanse as he could.

"Wow." Larry sipped some coffee from his travel mug, filled up at the Strawberry schoolhouse. The coffee was the only useful thing they'd found there.

"I figure we should book us a guide to take us down into the canyon," Larry said sipping the last of the coffee and sighing contentedly. "Some old sidewinder who knows every crook, nook, hook, and cranny of the canyon."

"How long does it take?"

"A day down and then a day back. Like I said, this hole is deeeeeep."

"So we camp?"

"Actually, we stay overnight at the Phantom Lodge."

"Phantom? You're kidding me."

"Nope. Don't worry. No ghosts. It's named after the otherworldly effect the setting sun has on the sky, or something like that. Let's go find a guide. Smell any horses?"

Neil sniffed the air and gagged. "Definitely. Over near that lodge."

They walked to the lodge and saw a corral. A wrinkled woman in a cowboy hat and worn jeans was pitching hay into a large trough. She took off her hat and wiped some sweat from her forehead as she watched the Flambés approach. She looked as tanned as leather.

"Well, lookie what we have here. A couple of city slickers."

Larry nodded. "We're looking for a valley."

The woman jerked her head toward the giant hole. "Done. That'll be fifty bucks."

"A specific valley," Neil said.

"Okay, why?"

Neil hesitated, but Larry jumped in with both feet. "We think it might be the location of a lost gold mine."

The woman raised an eyebrow. "I have been hiking these trails for longer than you two have been alive, put together . . . times three. There's some copper in the canyon, but no gold."

Neil deflated, but Larry shook the news off. "Sounds like the perfect place to keep a gold mine hidden."

The guide looked skeptical but gave a slow nod. "Maybe. Maybe. I've heard weirder tales that have turned out to be true. But there's lots of valleys to look at for miles and miles . . . and miles."

Larry tapped his phone and held up the photo of the map. "This is the specific valley. Look familiar?"

The woman took a long look at the picture, squinting to take in the details.

"There's a few down there that might be worth digging around. And there are some cliff dwellings way up the river valley, near a place called Nankoweap. Might be worth a look-see." She pointed east.

Neil's spirits rose, and he and Larry looked at each other and beamed. "That's even closer to the line between the fruits," Larry said.

"The what?" the woman said.

"Never mind. It's a chef thing. So, when can we start?" Neil said.

"Ever ridden a mule?"

Neil looked at Larry, who always seemed to have some experience doing just about anything and everything, and Larry didn't disappoint.

"Yes sirree, pardner. I've saddled up on some mule rides in the Rockies and even gone on trail rides with the great mule racer, Dawn Key."

The woman nodded, apparently impressed. "How about the redheaded kid here?"

Neil eyed the mules nervously. "Is it hard?"

"Depends on what you're referring to by 'it,'" she said with a wink. "But mules are very easy to get along with. Just sit tight and we'll get you both saddled up right enough. You're lucky it's not the busy season. You got any luggage?"

"We'll go get it and be right back," Larry said.

He and Neil walked to the parking lot.

"What did she mean by 'depends on what you're referring to'?" Neil asked.

Larry chuckled. "I'd suggest stuffing some extra padding in the seat of your pants."

"Oh."

As they approached the parking lot, Neil was sure he saw something move near the FrankenWagon. It was hard to tell with the shimmering of the sunlight on the asphalt, but it looked almost like a person that floated away.

"Did you see that?"

"See what?" Larry said.

"Never mind," Neil said, blinking and shaking his head.

They reached the van, but there was nobody close by. Neil reached for the handle and smelled saltpeter on the air. The smell was unmistakable.

He jerked his head quickly in the direction of the breeze and was sure he saw the distant figure of a man on a horse. He turned and tapped Larry on the shoulder. "Look over there," he said, pointing. But as soon as Neil looked back, the figure was gone.

"Oh, look! Mountains! Trees! Cacti!" Larry joked. "Did you just notice them?"

"Never mind." Neil frowned. "I'm going to get the cookbook out of the glove compartment, just in case." He was relieved to see the map was still there. He grabbed a heavy-duty freezer bag from the kitchen and tucked the book inside. Then he placed it in his backpack and stuffed some extra clothes around it, along with his favorite knife and a couple of guidebooks he'd borrowed from Julio.

He stepped out of the cab and locked his door, scanning the horizon for any sign, or smell, of the mysterious figure. But there was nothing.

Larry finally slid out of the van with two packed and obviously heavy duffel bags.

"Moving here?" Neil joked.

"Just being prepared," Larry said. "And mules can carry a house on their backs if they have to, so better safe than sorry. Let's go find us some treasure!"

CHAPTER THIRTEEN

PHANTOM

The guide was named Anna Silverheels, and she had been born and raised on the Hualapai Reservation, smack in the middle of the canyon. She said she was older than she looked.

"And you look ancient," Larry joked.

Neil flinched but Anna guffawed loudly.

"You got that right! I was here when the river was just a creek and the canyon was just a ditch," she called back. "Mind that bumpy bit in the trail there, ginger."

On cue, Neil's mule stumbled ever so slightly on a loose pile of rock. The mule was never in danger of falling, but the jolt sent a fresh throbbing ache straight into Neil's rear end. He'd already stopped once and put on four extra pairs of underwear and stuffed a T-shirt in his pants, but the three hours on the hard back of a mule, even with padding, had given Neil what Larry gleefully called "saddle bum."

"How much longer?" Neil called through gritted teeth.

"Almost at the lodge," Anna called. "You two should

have a nice cabin all to yourselves. And the food at the canteen is amazing."

Neil snorted before he could stop himself.

"What did you say?" Anna said. "You calling me a liar?"

Neil fought the urge to argue and lost the fight. "No, I'm sure the beans, beans, and beans at the 'canteen' are great."

Anna peered back over her shoulder. "I got my eye on you, ginger. There ain't a better steak for miles."

"It's also the only steak for miles," Neil said under his breath.

Larry chuckled. "Don't pay Slappy Neil no never mind, ma'am. He's a little chef back in the big smoke and he does sometimes get his chaps in a tizzy."

"Well, the cook at the canteen is a friend of mine. He's good at cookin' and he's a deadeye marksman, if you get my drift."

Neil decided it was best to keep quiet.

Despite his aching posterior, he had enjoyed the mule ride. Anna had pointed out dozens of amazing vistas, sounds, and plants. She pointed out a few edible cacti and flowers, too. Neil immediately began working out recipes.

"This place just kind of feels right, eh?" Larry called back over his shoulder.

"Yeah," Neil said. He thought the canyon was exactly the sort of place a homesick cook and a sociopathic army major could easily get lost during a storm. Neil had a good feeling about this. Strawberry hadn't been a total dead end. Peach Springs was close, and an imaginary line from there to Strawberry went right through the heart of their trip. There were so many valleys nearby that Neil was sure one of them would match the picture on Guillermo's map.

They were close to solving this mystery and saving Salsa Verde Ranch. He might even get back in time for the finale of the festival.

Of course, Neil also kept his ears and nose open the entire journey, nervously looking back each time a mule dislodged a stone or a lizard shot out from underneath a bush.

One other thing was bugging him. Isabella hadn't responded to his text of the picture of the canyon. They'd completely lost cell service about halfway down the side of the canyon, and Anna had told them they'd be out of contact, "roughing it" until they came back out a few days later. But he'd expected some response.

"Do you think Isabella is mad she can't be here?" Neil asked. "She should have landed by now."

Larry tried to set his mind at ease. "She's busy with her business, chef boy. Don't worry."

"Yeah, yeah. I know," Neil said.

"Well, you still have her 'Dear Ned' letters to look forward to when we get down to the ranch!"

They turned a corner and Neil saw a series of stone-and-log cabins. The smell of cooking steak and veggies reached his nose. It didn't stink. In fact, the steak smelled perfectly seared, almost nearing completion. Neil smiled

as he heard the faint sizzle of the meat being flipped onto a spitting-hot grill. There was even the slightest hint of smoking mesquite wood chips. He began to lick his lips.

Anna pulled out a cell phone. "I called ahead up top and told him to make ginger here some extra beans, beans, and beans."

"Sorry," Neil said. "It smells great."

"Apology accepted," Anna said. "Now let's tie up our mules and go settle in before we grab the grub."

Neil noted, happily, that the ten minutes it would take to settle in was exactly how long a steak like that should rest before being served.

Things were looking up.

Looking down, Neil saw the river churning next to him. He almost threw up the very excellent bacon and eggs

Ira Hayes, the cook at the Phantom Lodge, had served for breakfast.

"Remind me again why we're out here?" Neil called to Larry and Anna.

"The best way to see the valleys and the cave dwellings is to take a rafting trip along the river!" Anna yelled over the rushing water. She and Larry were sitting on opposite sides of a large yellow raft. They were using long yellow paddles to balance and steer the boat.

They'd taken a bus up the river, past Nankoweap Creek, and were now paddling back toward the lodge.

Neil was sitting on a bench in the middle and was keeping a lookout for any likely candidates.

"See anything?" Larry asked, looking even more like a wet, happy dog than usual.

"Not yet."

Many of the valleys along the river looked promising, and the closer they got to the cliff dwellings, the more they seemed to fit the map. But so far, nothing had been perfect.

"Hold on tight, everybody!" Anna called out suddenly.

The raft lurched around a bend and almost smashed into a huge mass of boulders. Anna and Larry paddled furiously. The boat veered slightly to the right and they slipped by. Larry yelled, "Whoopee!!!" at the top of his lungs. "That was AWESOME!!!!"

"More rapids ahead!" Anna hollered.

Neil gripped the supports of the bench tightly. The boat rocked from side to side. He forced himself to keep his eyes open.

"What's that?" he said, nodding his head toward a break in the canyon wall about a half mile ahead.

"That's where the cave dwellings are."

Neil and Larry exchanged glances.

"Keep your eyes peeled, like potatoes," Larry said.

The current carried them past high cliffs. Neil could see a smaller canyon stretching away into the distance, with a thinner line of water along the bottom.

"Nankoweap Creek," Anna called. "Look right?"

Neil shook his head.

The meeting of the two waters churned the river, and as they passed by, the nose of their boat rose and fell. They would rise higher than Neil thought possible on a river and then smash back down with incredible force. The spray soaked him to the bone, and despite the baking sun, he shivered.

Neil was starting to feel sick again, but on the tenth crest he saw it, a valley, set back into the canyon to their left.

"What's that?"

Anna pointed with her paddle. "Sixty-Mile Canyon."

Neil looked at the opening. The jagged floor and the high sides looked very close to the valley on Guillermo's map.

"Can we pull over?"

Anna turned and raised an eyebrow. It made her forehead look more craggy than the canyon. "In the middle of the rapids? Sure, if you want to drown! We'll pull up ahead and then hike back."

"More hiking?" Neil gave a groan that was audible even over the rushing water. His rear end and legs were still exhausted from the hours of mule riding and then hiking to the boat launch.

But he was relieved when they found a relatively calm spot in the river and pulled the boat up onto the rocky shore.

Neil threw off his life jacket, knelt down, and kissed the solid ground. He could still feel his head and body swaying back and forth.

"C'mon, you snakebit landlubber," Larry said, throwing Neil his pack.

Neil slung it over his shoulder, and they began walking the rocky shore along the riverside, a little too closely to the rushing water for Neil's liking.

"I hope my eyes weren't playing tricks on me," he said. They had been going by pretty quickly.

"I believe in ya," Larry said. "You've looked at Guillermo's map about a hundred times, so you've got a pretty good idea of what we're looking for."

"But there were some jagged rocks and stuff that weren't quite the same," Neil said. As he said this, he stepped on a loose rock. It slipped out from under him and cascaded down the side of the incline, splashing into the river. Larry reached out and grabbed Neil before he could follow the rock.

Anna pointed at disappearing ripples. "That could explain the difference. Erosion, landslides, rubble. This area is made of some particularly soft rock."

"Soft rock, that's what my dad listens to!" Larry started playing a riff on air guitar. The sound echoed off the canyon walls, sending a few crows into the air, cawing loudly. "Everyone's a critic," Larry said. "But I bet there have been lots of changes in the topography in the past century."

"Topo-what?" asked Neil.

"The way the land looks. You were suppose to study that in geography."

"Geo-what?"

Larry shook his head sadly and continued walking.

"I was just kidding on that last one," Neil said.

"Sure you were." Larry chuckled.

They reached the edge of Sixty-Mile Canyon. It was dwarfed by the main canyon but was still enormous. A sliver of a creek ran along the bottom.

"That's exactly the sort of creek that might turn into a river in a huge storm," Neil said.

Anna nodded. "It doesn't flood as badly here as it does in the desert, but the water levels can rise pretty fast."

The sound of the rushing rapids disappeared quickly as they walked, and it became incredibly still and quiet. Neil could hear birds singing and the breeze whooshing through the bushes and small trees that dotted the valley walls.

"How far do we need to go in?" Larry asked.

Neil pulled out his phone and called up a photo of the map. "Well, the X is over two boulders. I guess we have to find those."

Larry laughed as he took in the thousands of boulders on either side of the canyon walls.

"I guess we better start looking!" Larry said. "If we split up, we'll cover the whole thing before lunch!"

Anna looked skeptical. "Maybe. I'll head up the north

side," she said. "You and Slappy check out the south side. We'll see whether your two heads are better than mine."

"A race!" Larry said. "Cool!"

"Now *she's* calling me Slappy?" Neil said.

"Think of it as a term of affection," Anna said with a smile. Then she leaped the creek and started searching the canyon wall.

After an hour of scrambling and getting scratched up by cacti and dry branches, Neil and Larry were still empty-handed.

Neil sat down and took a swig of water from his canteen. He wiped the sweat off his forehead and gazed at the other valley wall. Anna was leaping around like a mountain goat, sure-footed and fast.

"Anna's making pretty fast progress on that side," Larry said.

"How do we know we can trust her?" Neil asked. "She could find the mine there, tell us she saw nothing, and then come back later and grab the thing for herself."

"Ah, she's fine. I even offered her some of the gold, if we find the place, but she said she has all the things she needs right here." Larry swept his hand across the rocks, the sky, and the gently babbling creek below.

Neil took a second to take it all in. "I guess I can understand that," he said. He took a deep breath and felt calm.

He also smelled something.

Bat poop.

He gave a start before realizing

there was no saltpeter in this aroma, just actual fresh and moist bat poop. He darted his head from side to side, trying to locate as accurately as possible the exact location.

Larry had seen Neil on a scent many times before. "What is it, boy? Smell something?"

Neil nodded. "Remember what Feleena said about the bats that led Guillermo out of the cave? I'm willing to bet that any cave with enough bats to lead a guy out safely will also have enough bat poop in it to stink up a storm."

Neil began walking among the boulders, homing in on the scent. After about ten minutes of stopping, smelling, and getting his bearings, he spied a giant rock halfway up the side. He sniffed. There was definitely a breeze from there with guano galore.

"I thought the map showed two boulders," Larry said.

"Maybe one fell down into the valley floor?" Neil asked. "But that's where the smell is coming from, and there's definitely something behind that rock."

Larry beamed. "Let's get up there and find us some gold!"

They walked closer and closer.

Neil was struck both by how improbable it was that they were right, but also by how many signs pointed to him being on the right track.

Even Larry could smell the bat poop as they sidled next to the rock. "Stinky!" he said. They began circling the huge rock, looking for a way behind.

"The smell is coming out near the top," Neil said. "Help me up."

Larry linked his fingers and made a loop for Neil's foot. He lifted his cousin up, and Neil grabbed the top of the rock.

"There's a hole!" he said. "There's no way you'd see that unless you were right on top of it."

"Hold tight, I'm coming up!" Larry took hold of Neil's leg.

"Ouch!" Neil hollered. "Assuming this is the right place, how did Guillermo get up here by himself?" he added as Larry struggled to pull himself up. With one final heave, he made it.

Larry sat next to Neil and examined the rubble down below. "I think this boulder has shifted down over the years, so the crack used to be lower."

"Should we head inside?" Neil said with a mix of trepidation and excitement.

"Tell Anna," Larry said.

Neil stood up to call Anna. "I don't see her."

Larry shielded his eyes with his hand. "She must be searching behind some rocks," he said. "Let's go look around inside. If it is the right cave, we can come back out and find her."

Neil nodded. He turned. Out of the corner of his eye he saw something move, a dark shadow on the farthest rim of the canyon. He turned and peered to get a better look, but all he saw was the unmoving silhouette of a large cactus.

"C'mon, cuz! It's cool down here." Larry had already slipped down in through the crack.

"Coming," Neil said. He slipped off the back of the boulder and into the cave.

CHAPTER FOURTEEN

CRACKED

Larry flicked on a flashlight up ahead and shone it on the walls. "There is a hole back here that goes down, just like in the legend."

"Can you see anything at the bottom?"

Larry leaned over. "I can't even see the bottom. It's dark, and pretty deep. Guillermo must have fallen for weeks."

"So what do we do?"

"I have a rope in my duffel bag."

"Long enough?"

"Duh. I'm always prepared, remember?"

"What do you need me to do?"

"Find a good place to tie it off, and then we'll go down and see what we can find."

Neil took the rope, found a sturdy rock, and tied a

secure knot. He yanked on it to make sure it could take Larry's weight. He was no amateur. He'd tied knots that could keep a hundred-pound roast packed together during hours of sweltering oven braising. This knot would not come loose.

"Ready," he called.

Larry gave a thumbs-up, clutched the flashlight in his teeth, and began his descent.

Neil crouched by the edge, watching the light grow fainter and fainter. "You good?" he called.

"Yeah. The smell is getting stronger and stronger," Larry called, his voice echoing up the sides of the hole. "And by that I mean worse and worse."

"Welcome to my world, every time you make an omelette," Neil called.

"Ha-ha! Wait . . . whoa. I'm at the bottom. This is cool!"

"What?" Neil called.

There was no answer.

"Larry?"

Still no answer.

Neil stood up and called louder. "LARRY??"

He grabbed the rope and started to pull. It was completely slack. He gripped the rope between his feet and slid down as slowly as he could. Even still, his hands began to burn from the friction. He could see what Larry had meant about the smell of bat poop growing stronger and stronger. It was almost overwhelming.

Finally, his heart racing, he reached the bottom. His feet began to sink into the soft ground. It wasn't dirt, he realized.

There was no light anywhere. Neil, in his panic, had stupidly left his backpack and flashlight up top. "Larry!" he called.

A light flashed on the cave wall to his right. "Hey, Neil!"

"What do you mean, 'Hey, Neil'? Why didn't you answer me?"

"Answer you when?"

"I was calling down the hole."

"Weird. I didn't hear anything once I stepped away from the bottom. Acoustics, man, they are so bizarre."

Neil suddenly realized where he was standing. Larry's flashlight glowed off the walls, glittering like a night sky. "So, is this Guillermo's cave? It is, right?"

Larry shrugged and was not smiling. "I don't see any gold, pardner, sorry."

Neil was confused. He pointed at the wall. "But what's all this? This cave must be worth millions!"

Larry shook his head. "Remember my geologist friend from the college?"

"Petra Stone?"

Larry nodded. "Well, we went spelunking lots of times."

"Spell . . . what?"

"Spelunking. I know! Supercool word. It means 'cave exploring.' Anyway, we found lots of pyrite, which is what all this is. Not gold. Fool's gold."

Neil couldn't believe it. The sparkling walls were beautiful.

"This isn't gold?"

"Nope."

"So Guillermo's cave is a fake?"

Larry shook his head again. "No way anyone would have been fooled by pyrite, even back then. Guillermo bought that ranch with some real gold. My take? This isn't his cave."

Neil's shoulders sagged. He'd been so sure they were right.

"But we're not totally off track. This place is connected to the legend, in a big way."

Neil was completely confused now, and it wasn't just the off-gassing from the giant mound of bat poop. "How?"

"Follow me."

Larry led Neil into a smaller room, a low-ceilinged offshoot from the main cave. Inside the walls glowed with yet more pyrite. There, in the middle of the room, was what looked like a sleeping person. Neil gave a start. "Who is that?"

"The question is, who *was* that," Larry said, kneeling down. "This is just a pile of bones and rags now. And other things." He picked up a tarnished brass button from the rib cage of the remains. Neil could also see a rusted revolver lying next to the hip. The leather holster had long since rotted away.

Larry handed the button to Neil. "These are buttons from an army uniform. Late nineteenth century, if I'm not wrong. And there are initials carved into the handle of that revolver. MTG."

Neil felt a shiver run down his spine, and the hairs on his arms stood up straight. "What are you saying?"

"This here is what's left of Major Theodore Gravestone Graves."

Neil might have imagined it, but he was sure he felt a cool breeze come through the tunnel. He turned involuntarily and was almost as certain that a shadow moved across the back wall of the room.

His mouth felt dry as he spoke. "So, what does that mean?"

"Well, at the very least it means that Gravestone also thought this was the lost mine. He died here, that's pretty clear."

"But what . . ." Neil stopped. He wasn't sure what to make of anything now. "Did he think he'd found Guillermo's gold mine, but there was no gold?"

His thoughts were interrupted by a sound. It was the sound of a rope slapping against bat poop. The knot he'd made was secure enough to let two young men climb down. How had it come loose?

Neil rushed back to the hole.

The rope lay like a coiled snake. It hadn't come loose. It had been cut, the ragged end lying on top of the pile.

Neil looked up the hole. "Who's there?"

No answer.

"Who's THERE? ANSWER ME!"

Neil thought he heard shuffling feet and even, possibly, a laugh.

He craned his neck. A slight breeze did come down the hole. It carried no voice but did bring Neil's nose the faintest aroma of saltpeter.

CHAPTER FIFTEEN

GUANO GO

"So now what do we do?" Neil asked, sitting on the rope. "We could try climbing back up. There were some handholds on the walls. Well, sort of."

Neil shone the flashlight up the dark expanse of the hole. There were a few outcroppings along the way, but not many. "Unless you've grown extendable arms, I'm not sure that's actually a good idea."

"Okay," Larry said. He wasn't really paying much attention. He was using a stick to draw something in the bat poop.

"Didn't the legend say Guillermo found another way out of the cave?"

"We've already established this isn't the same cave."

"But maybe there's still an exit?"

"It doesn't look like Gravestone ever found a way out." Larry gestured back over his shoulder to the smaller room off the back.

"Is this supposed to make me feel better?" Neil stood up and paced in the muck. He wanted to punch something. "Do you think Anna was the one who trapped us down here?"

"I doubt it. Of course, it's possible. But why would she?"

"For the gold."

"There isn't any gold."

"But she doesn't know that, does she?" Neil paced back and forth, his feet more and more covered in bat poop. "Maybe she thinks we found the mine. She leaves us to die down here and then she comes back and claims the gold."

"Everyone back at the lodge saw her leave with us this morning. Pretty suspicious, isn't it?"

"Maybe they're all in cahoots."

"Cahoots?" Larry stared at Neil, a smile spreading across his stubbly face.

"Yes, cahoots."

Larry began to laugh so hard he almost fell over.

"What's so funny? You've been using cowboy slang the entire time we've been here."

"Yeah, but when I say it, it sounds cool. You just sound dorky. Anyway, it would take a lot of track covering for Anna to convince the cops she lost us, with no trace."

"Isn't track covering one of her skills?"

Larry just sighed and went back to drawing in the poop.

"I left my backpack up top," Neil said. "The map was inside. I feel like such a jerk. That was the only link Julio and Feleena had to their past, especially if the ranch gets sold."

"We've been in worse pickles than this," Larry said. He stood up and threw away the stick.

Neil looked at the writing Larry had made in the poop. *Feleena: If you find us dead, this isn't the right mine. No gold here, just ghosts*, he read. "Nice, Larry. That's very helpful."

"Just trying to make sure we leave a message," Larry said. "It's like those carvings all those condemned prisoners left on the walls of the Tower of London."

Neil had seen dozens of carved "last words" on their recent trip to London. Warnings, confessions, and prayers left on the walls of the prison.

"Do you think Gravestone might have had the same idea?" Neil wondered.

"That's a very good question," Larry said. "Let's go find out."

Neil felt another chill as he approached Gravestone's bones and uniform. They were laid down in an almost relaxed position. "It's like he lay down for a rest and never woke up."

"Maybe he knew he was going to die and just gave up."

They began to search the walls for any sign of markings or carvings. They found nothing. "If Gravestone had any last thoughts, he took them with him when he died," Larry said. He took out his phone and began snapping multiple pictures of the scene.

Neil took a closer look at the revolver. He knelt

down and sniffed. Faintly, mixed with all the other smells of the cave, was saltpeter-based gunpowder. It was almost indistinguishable from the gunpowder he'd been smelling for days. Were they being haunted by the ghost of this cruel army major? Had he led them here? To their deaths?

Neil knew the idea was crazy. He lifted up the revolver and flipped open the chamber. All the bullets were still there.

"I guess he didn't die in a gunfight," Neil said.

Maybe, like Neil and Larry, he'd come down here thinking he'd found the lost mine, then gotten trapped and had just given up on life?

Neil's thoughts were shaken by a sound from back underneath the hole.

Loose stones tumbled down and bounced off the coiled rope.

Larry and Neil ran back and stood under the hole.

"Halloooooo!" called a woman's voice.

"Anna!" Larry said. "Is that you?"

"Of course it's me, you blue-gilled son of a catfish. There was a small rockslide on my side, and a rock conked me a good one upside the head. When I woke up, with a splitting headache, I noticed you two had disappeared."

"I told you she was good people," Larry said.

"So how did you find us?" Neil called.

Anna snorted. "I guide dim-witted tourists for a living! I've tracked toddlers who followed hares down holes, hipsters who tried hiking the canyon blindfolded, and even one incredibly clue-less couple from San Francisco who tried to shoot the rapids on surfboards. Finding you two was a walk in the national park."

"How do we get out of here?" Neil called.

"There's no other exit I can see from up here. Too bad all the bats are hibernating, or they might lead you out through some cracks."

"I had wondered about the bat-poop-to-actual-bat ratio," Larry said. "I had this scary image of a really big bat with stomach problems."

"Thanks for sharing." Neil shook his head to try to dislodge the image. It didn't work.

"Let's get you two out of there and then we can talk about what the heck is really going on," Anna called. "I'm going to throw down a rope. Just give me a minute to tie it off a little better than you did."

Neil was offended. "I tied a great knot! Someone cut it."

Anna didn't say anything for a minute. When she did speak, there was no inkling she was kidding.

"In that case, it wasn't a person who did it. There's no evidence anyone else has been in here but me and you two."

CHAPTER SIXTEEN

RAPID FIRE

Anna had searched and searched the cave opening and seen no evidence of anyone else. There were no traces of frayed rope ends. No footprints. No trace of anyone having been there between the Flambés and Anna. And Neil's backpack hadn't been moved. He happily opened the cookbook to see the map securely held inside. Had the rope just been weak, ready to break? If so, he and Larry were lucky they hadn't fallen down the hole.

Neil ran through the dizzying facts during their hike back out of the canyon.

Every bit of evidence had pointed to this as the lost cave. His instincts had been right.

But?

No gold.

No skillet.

They'd found what was very likely the remains of Gravestone. Had he also thought this was the right cave? Why hadn't he just left?

There was no evidence anyone else had ever been inside, between Gravestone's death and Neil and Larry's brief scare.

So, following the fruits hadn't been a crazy idea. Neil had been right.

But he'd also been wrong. This wasn't the cave.

Was Guillermo's map a misdirection?

Was this literally a dead end?

They reached the raft.

"You say it was a rockslide that knocked you out?" Larry asked as he and Anna shoved off from the shore.

"They happen a lot, especially after a few weeks of freezing and thawing. Lots of loose stones around. I shoulda been more alert." She rubbed the bump on her head. "Anyway, the sooner we start paddling, the sooner we'll get back to the lodge."

"Great! I'm starving." Larry opened up his duffel bag and pulled out a giant thermos. Neil could see at least two more inside.

Larry unscrewed the gap and guzzled a large mouthful of dark coffee. "Always prepared."

Neil shook his head. Looking ahead, he saw the canyon narrow. The water also began to change color. A light green was mixing with the darker waters of the main river. Neil also noticed, with some alarm, that the water was churning.

"What's that?"

"The confluence of the Little Colorado River with the Colorado," Anna said. "It will get a bit choppy as we shoot through that narrow section, so hold on tight."

Neil put on his backpack, worried it would get tossed out by the waves. Then he gripped the sides of the bench as the raft began to lift and fall, worried *he* would get tossed out by the waves.

As they passed through the narrow chasm between two peaks, the nose of the raft rose and Neil smelled something—saltpeter. He looked up and saw a figure, standing on the top of a giant stone.

It was a man, dressed in a flowing cape, with large dark boots, wearing a black hat. He was standing with his legs apart, pointing something down at the raft.

"Gravestone?" Neil whispered.

Something whizzed past his ear, like a bee had flown near his head. He heard the sound of air escaping. Another bee and then more air escaping.

"The raft is leaking!" Anna yelled.

One more bee flew past Neil and into the raft. He looked up. The man holstered his gun and then slipped out of sight.

Neil could hear Anna and Larry furiously paddling to keep the raft from being crushed by the rapids. He could also feel the raft losing its shape. His shock now gave way to panic. He had a life jacket on, but one look at the water convinced him it wouldn't be enough.

"Abandon ship!" Anna yelled.

Neil turned and saw Larry smiling. Smiling?

"Always prepared," Larry said. He reached into his duffel bag and pulled out two small oxygen tanks with scuba masks.

He gave one to Anna, who put the tank and mask on just as a wave flipped her over the side of the raft and into the water.

In a flash Larry put the other mask over Neil's head, grabbed him, and then fell into the river. Neil grabbed the straps of Larry's life jacket as they bobbed violently in the rapids. Larry held on to Neil, and Neil held on to Larry. They sped past a line of boulders. The water rushed faster as it was forced together between the stones, and Neil felt the full weight push him and Larry under the surface.

Neil was spinning, but he managed to keep a grip on Larry. The water drove him down to the bottom and sharp stones dug into his shoulder, but he would not let go.

He kicked with all his might to fight the undertow, feeling Larry going limp. Neil could breathe, but he realized in a panic that Larry was drowning.

He kicked harder and harder for the surface. He broke through. Larry's head bobbed ominously to the side. He had a gash on his forehead, and it was bleeding. The water was calming but was still violent. Neil quickly took out his mouthpiece and slipped it into Larry's mouth.

"Breathe!" he said, and a splash of water filled his throat.

Neil had to fight to inhale as each wave seemed to fill his mouth just as he'd spat out the water from the last. He began to hyperventilate, and Larry was still not breathing.

Neil let go of Larry's vest and wrapped his arms around his cousin's ribs. He used what little strength and time he had left to squeeze Larry repeatedly. Larry's head blocked some of the waves, and Neil was able to draw in some air. He squeezed and squeezed as the river began to calm, carrying them slowly now.

Was it too late?

The limp remains of their raft drifted by, followed by a line of Larry's coffee-filled thermoses.

With a loud cough Larry spat up a large amount of water. His chest heaved as he gave huge gasping breaths. Neil struggled to keep the mouthpiece on Larry, who for some reason kept trying to rip it off. Neil had heard of drowning people who panicked.

With a push Larry got free from Neil and lunged for the closest thermos. In one swift move he unscrewed the cap and took a swig.

"Ahhhhhhh," he croaked. "Better than oxygen."

"Over here!" said a distant voice. Anna had washed up on the far shore and was waving her hands back and forth.

"We must have hit some rocks back there," Larry said as they dog-paddled toward her. "Something punctured the raft bottom."

119

"It wasn't rocks. It was . . . I think it was Gravestone."

"So you hit your head too?" Larry said.

"I know it sounds crazy, but there was a man on the rocks. He looked just like Gravestone. And he shot at us and sank the raft."

They watched the raft disappear down the river, sinking as the water leaked into the pontoons. "I guess we'll never know for sure," Larry said.

Neil stared back down the river to where the man had stood. He had seen him. The man had shot at them. Neil was sure of it.

They reached Anna, and Neil told her what he'd seen.

"I don't doubt what you think you saw," she said. "But I don't know how anybody could stand there, shoot at me three times without me noticing, and then vanish."

Neil was tempted to say, *What if he was a ghost*, but decided not to. Maybe he had seen things. It wasn't that he doubted his eyes. It was more that the possibility was too surreal to accept. Thinking he was wrong was easier.

"So, how do we get back to camp?"

Anna pointed at the rocky shoreline. "Walk."

Neil could feel the weight of the oxygen tank in his backpack. He felt a moment of annoyance, then shame. This tank had saved his life. Larry's stupid scuba gear had saved his life.

He put an arm on Larry's shoulder. "Always be prepared," he said.

Larry nodded. "And that wasn't even the emergency I had in mind! I figured we'd need it in the desert." Then he reached down and picked up Anna's tank. "Who knows, we still might."

CHAPTER SEVENTEEN

RATTLED SNAKE

Walking took a lot longer than rafting, and it was well past suppertime by the time they reached the lodge.

Anna shouted, "I ain't smellin' any steaks grillin'," as they reached the path to the house. Her voice boomed off the canyon walls.

Chef Hayes peeked his head out of the dining room window. "I expected you back hours ago! What happened?"

Anna waved him off. "That would take longer than a cactus's lifespan to explain. Let's just say we had it all. A rockslide, leaky raft, bat poop, bad rope, and possibly a ghost."

Chef Hayes raised an eyebrow but seemed to take the explanation in stride. "Well, you go get clean and I'll fire up the grills."

A short time later,

showered and exhausted, they sat down on a wooden bench, in front of a spread of hanger steaks, roasted root vegetables, and crusty corn bread.

Neil, Larry, and Anna wolfed it all down without saying a word.

"That was excellent," Neil said as he leaned back against the wall, completely stuffed and completely worn out. "I'm looking forward to a good night's sleep."

"No appetite for dessert?" Hayes called out from the kitchen. Neil didn't hear him. He'd already fallen into a deep sleep.

Neil awoke to the sound of an old-fashioned telephone ringing. Larry was leaning on his shoulder, snoring. Neil looked around the dining room. The lights were all dimmed. The tables had all been cleaned and wiped down.

Neil could hear Chef Hayes in the kitchen, lifting the phone off its receiver.

Anna wasn't sitting next to them. She must have gone to bed.

Neil couldn't hear the phone conversation. Hayes lowered his voice, as if he wanted to make sure he wasn't overheard.

Neil craned his head. He heard a click as Hayes hung up the phone. Then he heard footsteps as Anna walked back into the dining room from outside, closing the door quietly behind her.

Chef Hayes stuck his head out of the kitchen and waved her over quickly.

Neil closed his eyes and listened.

"Anna, that was the police."

"What do *they* want?" Anna didn't exactly sound impressed.

"Those two. They said that . . ." Hayes lowered his voice to a whisper, and Neil missed the rest.

"That's the stupidest thing I've ever heard. Those two couldn't even get themselves out of a hole in the ground."

"Well, the police are asking us to keep an eye on them until morning. They'll send down some officers first thing."

"Did you tell them I was here?"

"Nope," Hayes said. "Why?"

"Never mind. Just don't mention my name, no matter what happens. You hear?"

The kitchen door closed and Neil could hear Anna breathing. She didn't move for a long while. When she did, she walked quietly over to Neil and shook his shoulder.

"Slappy. Time for you to head back to your cabin. Ira's gotta close up the dining room." Then she added in a lower voice, "You and your cousin pack up everythin' you hold dear and meet me by the mules in five minutes. Now act calm." She got up and walked out the door.

Neil nodded and stretched his arms dramatically. Larry raised his head and smiled.

"Time to go," Neil said. He leaned in close to Larry and whispered, "Red Corn in the Kettle."

Larry's eyes popped open. This was one of the code phrases they used in the kitchen when something odd was up, like a food critic was dining in disguise, or an inspector was about to walk into the kitchen while Larry was juggling eggs.

"Bad?"

"I'll explain in a minute." They walked back to their cabin, trying to look calm and casual.

They quietly packed up the remaining oxygen tanks, the map, and their clothes. Then Neil turned off the light and peeked out through the window. Chef Hayes closed up the dining room and walked to his cabin. Neil waited a minute, and then he and Larry slipped out the window in the bathroom, just in case the chef was watching their door.

Anna was waiting for them by the mules. She was stroking their muzzles, doing her best to keep them quiet. A gas lamp lay on the ground, giving everything a kind of eerie golden glow.

"What's happening?" Neil whispered as she took their bags and strapped them on the backs of the mules.

"The cops say you two are wanted for attempted murder. That's all I know. They're coming for you in the morning."

"WHAT!?!" Neil said, shocked.

"Shhhhh," Anna said. "Ira is a good man and I don't want him getting in any trouble. But neither of you has the look of a killer."

"We're not!" Neil said.

Anna nodded. "But Ira's been told to keep you here. I'm going to get you out of here without him seeing a thing. That way he doesn't get in trouble."

"Won't you?" Larry asked.

Anna smiled. "I'll lie low for a spell. Then you two need to do me a favor."

"What?"

"I'm taking a big risk. Once you clear your names, tell the cops I didn't know anything. That you escaped without my help."

"What if we don't clear our names?" Larry asked.

"Well then, in a week I'll emerge from the cave where you tied me up and tell them you threatened to kill me too if I didn't help you. Sorry about that, but I've got to cover my tracks to stay in this business, and this place."

Larry held out his hand and shook Anna's. "Deal."

Riding in full daylight had been harrowing. Riding up the side of the canyon with only the moon to light the way was bloodcurdling. Every bush and cactus looked like a ghostly gunslinger, and Neil kept expecting to hear the sound of a phantom revolver.

The sun was a sliver on the horizon as they reached the rim of the canyon.

Neil and Larry took their bags. Neil sniffed the air, expecting to catch the smell of saltpeter. But the coast seemed to be clear.

"I guess we better get a move on," Neil said.

"Thanks for everything, you old mountain woman you," Larry said.

Anna smiled and turned her mule back toward the canyon. "Oh, I almost forgot." She gave a little laugh. "You guys fell asleep so quick after dinner you missed

Ira's amazing dessert. He told me to save you some."

She reached into her saddlebag and pulled out a foil-wrapped package and an envelope. "Skillet cake. Just the way my granddad used to make it when we went out on trail rides." She handed Larry the package.

"And he told me to give you the recipe," she said, handing it to Neil.

He took the envelope with a lump in his throat. "Why are you all being so nice to us?" he said.

Anna laughed. "I like you two. That's what friends do. Now get moving, and you better lie as low as a snake in a gully, if you know what's good for ya."

Then she kicked her heels into the mule and they clopped off into the canyon.

Neil turned to Larry. "I guess our best bet is to get back to Salsa Verde and see what the heck is going on."

"Well, pardner, let's get in the FrankenWagon and get the heck out of here."

CHAPTER EIGHTEEN

ABANDON SHIP

The FrankenWagon rocked and rolled across the desert floor. Larry did his best to control the bulk of the hybrid truck.

Once the sun had come up, Neil knew they were in the *most* identifiable vehicle in the entire state, possibly the entire United States. So he suggested Larry find an "alternate route" back to the Verde ranch.

Larry had turned off the road at the first chance and was now bombing over what looked like an overgrown hiking trail. Cacti and bushes sped by on either side. Neil hoped they weren't throwing too much dust into the air.

He also noticed with alarm that the last sign he'd seen on the road had said SKULL VALLEY, 30 MILES.

"Who named the places in this state? Zombies?"

Now that they were back in cell phone range, Larry

turned on his phone. It immediately began buzzing like a nest of angry wasps.

"That's a lot of voice mails," Larry said, watching his phone flip and flop on the top of the dashboard. "See what's up."

Neil grabbed the phone and went to the voice mails. There were at least a dozen calls, all from Feleena, and they painted a disturbing picture of what had happened while Neil and Larry had been hiking the canyon.

"You'd better have a listen," Neil said. He put the phone on speaker and played the messages in sequence.

BEEP. "Neil, Larry. There's trouble. Two of the chefs from the festival are in the hospital. The chief of police is a man named Joseph Aprende. You may have heard of him, a very strange man. My father calls him a throwback to the olden days. He has traced the poisoning back to a jar of barbecue sauce. I'll let you know what he says."

BEEP. "Aprende says the poisonous sauce is the one you left behind. It had traces of nightshade in it. The chefs are really sick. One is even being kept in an artificial coma. Please call me as soon as you get this."

BEEP. "Good news and bad news. The chefs are doing better. I've told the authorities it's impossible that you would try to kill anyone, but Sheriff Aprende is convinced you're guilty and he's vowing to come after you with a posse. He is a crazy man, and he is a great tracker."

BEEP. Feleena spoke in a hushed tone, as if she were holding the phone close and whispering. Neil could hear raised voices in the background. Two men were having some kind of argument. "Sheriff Aprende is fighting with my father. My father has told him you are on your way to California. He called my father a liar and threatened to send him to jail!"

BEEP. "We are all in so much trouble!" Feleena's voice was trembling. "A horrible man has come to the ranch. His name is Hector Whippet. He has a paper from the bank. It says he has paid off the debt for the ranch. He is now our landlord. If we don't pay him immediately, he will close us down! I told him I can't pay the rent. He told me I must pay the rent!"

BEEP. "Larry, Neil, we need your help! But if you come here, you will be arrested on sight, or worse. Aprende has left armed men hidden around the ranch with orders to bring you in, dead or alive."

BEEP. Feleena spoke in a calm, even voice. "Everything is fine here. Please come back."

The next message was from a different, unrecognized number.

BEEP. "I am so sorry. DO NOT COME BACK. Aprende said if I helped lure you here, he would convince Whippet to give us one more week to raise the money. We need that time. I am so sorry. I must go. He is coming."

Then, one more call from Feleena's cell.

BEEP. "Everything is fine here. Please come back. We are going to have a big party. See you soon."

Neil turned off the speaker and gave a long, low sigh. "So I guess we're on the run."

Larry smiled. "Dead or alive! I wonder if they'll make up those cool posters and tack them onto trees and stuff!

I wonder what the reward will be?"

Neil kicked the dashboard. "I sealed those bottles myself. There was nothing poisonous in them at all. Someone spiked them after we left."

Larry continued to visualize his very own Wanted poster. "I wonder if they'll make me look mean? Like with a desperado mustache!"

"Can you please be serious? We are in trouble."

"You got that right. I saw a TV story about this Aprende dude once. He's a total wingnut."

"Total?"

"He carries old six-shooters, wears a cowboy hat and spurs. He named his gun Lorelei or something like that. He believes in chain gangs. He wears a tin badge and rides a horse."

"Feleena called him a 'throwback.'"

"More like a throw-up," Larry said. "And I think we may have discovered the true identity of your Gravestone Ghost. OOooooooooHHHHHoooooooo. Spoooooky. A throw-up in a cowboy hat."

"All right, I get it."

"Look, I haven't even seen the guy, so maybe it is a ghost. . . . Nah, it's Aprende. He's using old-fashioned gunpowder in his old-fashioned six-shooter."

Neil sulked for a while, but he was also thinking

about everything he'd just learned. "The timing is still bugging me. Feleena's first call was only two days ago, after we went into the canyon."

"So?"

"I've been smelling the gunpowder since we left Pick-Me-Up. The other chefs hadn't even opened the sauce yet. Why would Aprende have been trailing us then?"

"I can think of a few reasons, and none of them are good." Larry steered the FrankenWagon into a small grassy culvert. "This looks pretty secluded. Time to sit and talk this out for a bit. I also need to brew up some fresh coffee."

Neil sat in his seat, tapping his finger on his upper lip.

Larry slipped into the back and began making his coffee, singing some cowboy ballad about being shot and falling in love, and stealing some cattle.

If only to save himself from hearing the song, Neil began to throw questions at Larry.

"If the saltpeter smell was from Aprende's gun, then why was he trailing us days *before* anyone had been poisoned?"

"Maybe he knew you were going to poison somebody, so he was getting a head start on the investigation."

"I didn't poison anybody!"

"I believe you! Unless the reward is really big. Then I'll turn you in."

"You are an idiot. Next question. If he already knew where we

131

were—remember, I also smelled saltpeter in Strawberry and the Grand Canyon—then why order Julio to say where we were heading?"

"Dunno," Larry said, walking back to the cab with a fresh pot of coffee. "Maybe it is a ghost who's been following us."

Larry leaped into his seat and took a sip from his mug, sighing contentedly. "Of course, if it was Aprende shooting at us on the river, he was trying pretty hard to make it look like a drowning accident."

"How did he get from Salsa Verde to the Grand Canyon so fast? I thought he rode a horse."

"He probably does that for show. I'll bet he's not above taking a car, or a helicopter or a plane for that matter, if it helps him catch a felonious fugitive."

"So Aprende has been following us for days. And wants us dead."

"I'm willing to bet he and this Whiplash character are working together to get the ranch."

Neil snapped his fingers. "That's it. If we don't find the mine, they get the ranch."

"But then Aprende followed us into the canyon. He sees us go into the cave and then figures we *did* find the mine, so he decides to let us die inside. Feleena and Julio never get their gold, so Whippet gets the ranch!"

"Then Aprende comes back to the canyon and 'discovers' the lost mine later."

"But he sees us escape from the mine, then decides we should 'drown' and tries to make it look like an accident."

Neil pursed his lips, angry. "I wonder if he realized it wasn't a real gold mine."

"I don't think he would have tried to drown us if he'd known that. He'd keep trying to track us. He was as convinced as we were that we'd found the right spot."

"Let's keep that info to ourselves for now," Neil said. He rolled down his window a crack and smelled. "He's probably tracking us now. I'll keep a lookout."

"You mean a smell-out."

"Whatever." Neil wrapped himself in a blanket and settled in. "I'll make us some lunch in a bit, once I've . . ." The events of the week, combined with their late-night flight out of the canyon, had left him completely exhausted.

"You want some of Hayes's skillet cake?" Larry asked.

But Neil didn't hear. He was fast asleep.

He was woken up a short time later by the sound of gunshots and the squealing of the FrankenWagon's wheels.

CHAPTER NINETEEN

FIGHT OR FLIGHT

The smell of vintage gunpowder and smoke hung thickly in the air. A small pebble smacked Neil in the forehead. He saw, with alarm, that the front windshield had been shattered.

"What's going on?"

"Aprende snuck up on us when you were sleeping and started blasting. I don't think he's alone, either."

Larry expertly swung the FrankenWagon through a narrow passage between two stone columns. Neil heard bullets strike the stone around them, sending bits of debris flying into the cab.

"Ouch!" Neil said as shards of stone bit into his face. A cut above his eye began to bleed. The blood, ever-growing dust cloud, and shards of stone were making it almost impossible to keep his eyes open. Larry was blinking constantly, trying to see where he was heading.

"Get the scuba masks!" Larry yelled. He gunned the engine and the FrankenWagon flew across an exposed field. They seemed to be heading farther and farther into the desert.

Neil scurried back into the trailer and grabbed the masks from Larry's duffel bag. He put one on and then rushed back, leaning against the boxes to keep his balance. Larry was still blinking and using his sleeve to wipe the dust from his face. Neil quickly placed the mask over Larry's head.

"Thanks," Larry said. "Better buckle up fast! We're about to hit a speed bump."

"In the desert?"

Neil looked up. There, straight in front of them, was a man on a horse. The same man who had shot out the raft in the canyon, Neil was sure of it.

Larry barreled toward him, actually increasing his speed.

"You're going to hit him!" Neil yelled, falling into his seat.

"If it's the ghost of Gravestone, we'll go right through him," Larry said.

"And if he doesn't get out of the way?" Neil asked, fumbling to hitch his buckle into the snap.

"Then he'll soon be the ghost of Sheriff Joe Aprende."

The horse tapped its hooves nervously and turned to run, but the man yanked the reins and held it still. They were now just yards apart. In seconds there would be a horrible collision.

Neil saw the face of the man for the first time. His

eyes were like dark pits. His mouth was set in a thin line. He showed no emotion as he waited for the Flambés to get closer. Neil watched in horror as the man calmly raised his right hand and pointed his pistol at the cab of the FrankenWagon.

"Duck!" Larry yelled.

Neil dipped his head just as Larry yanked the steering wheel to the left. Neil heard the sound of exploding glass as a bullet hit his passenger-side door. Bits of the window rained down on his back.

Larry sat back up and fought to keep the vehicle from tipping over. The FrankenWagon swayed dangerously from side to side as Larry held tightly to the wheel. Boxes and pots flew around the trailer. It was like shooting the rapids again, but on dry land.

Finally the oscillating stopped, and Larry went back to dealing with the bumpy terrain.

"That was close," Neil said. "Nice driving."

"Thank Marleen Aklavik, that ice-road trucker I traveled with a bit last winter. She taught me a lot." Larry gunned the engine again. "See if we're being followed."

Neil poked his head out of his window and saw Aprende receding into the background. His horse wasn't moving, and he seemed content to watch the FrankenWagon disappear into the wasteland.

Neil was sure he saw the man raise his head and laugh as another rider pulled up alongside.

Neil sat back in his seat, confused. "Why aren't they chasing us?"

Larry didn't say anything. He just pointed straight

ahead, and then up. The land was growing drier and drier, the plants more sparse. The blazing sun was high in the sky. Neil could already feel his skin beginning to bake and burn.

"So not only are we heading straight into the middle of the hottest place on planet Earth," Larry said, "we also don't have enough gas to get through to the other side."

"If we turn back, he'll be waiting."

Larry nodded. "And look at my cell phone."

Neil held up the phone and watched the service bars drop from four to zero in a matter of seconds.

"Aprende chased us in here on purpose."

Larry nodded.

"We're going to die, aren't we?"

Larry shook his head. "No, but the Frankie is." He sniffled and stroked the dashboard.

Neil nodded. "We've got to ditch her."

"And then we have to keep going. She's too easy to see from the sky. And you probably picked up the smell of the melting rubber tires."

Neil had certainly smelled that. The FrankenWagon was not an off-road vehicle. She was barely an on-road vehicle. He was starting to realize just how desperate their situation was. "We'll have to head out on foot."

"Yup. And hope like heck that we can survive long enough to get out of here alive."

Neil watched as the ground in front of them shimmered in the blazing heat. He also remembered what Julio had said about the desert. *Brutally hot at noon and close to freezing at midnight.* They'd need blankets, water, and food.

"We'll have to carry a lot of stuff," Neil said.

"Pack only essentials. Food, water."

Neil nodded at Larry. "And scuba gear."

CHAPTER TWENTY

JUST DESERTS

So there is definitely no ghost," Neil said. He knew he was trying to reassure himself. The sun had gone down and the sky was a tapestry of shining dots. Things were moving all around them, making slithering, whistling, and shuffling noises.

"He was real enough, and so were his bullets," Larry said. "And that's spookier than some dead guy, quite frankly."

The FrankenWagon had run out of gas, and tire rubber, at high noon in the middle of nowhere. Larry had used the last of the truck's momentum to guide her into

a dry creek bed. They grabbed as much as they could salvage and then began walking across the desert.

Larry had suggested a Viking funeral, burning the van on the spot, but Neil had convinced him that setting off a giant fireball was not the best way to lie low.

"In every movie I've seen, the guys who are lost in the desert want to get rescued," Larry said as they shuffled along. "I guess we're the exception."

"If we're found, we'll get turned over to Aprende."

"Who doesn't seem interested in hearing our side of the story."

"We've got to get out of here without being caught, find the mine, and then clear our names."

"So we just keep going straight." Neil and Larry looked at the vast expanse that spread out ahead of them and started walking. They didn't have a choice, Neil figured.

If Aprende were following them, he'd be coming from the way they came. They had a head start, thanks to the last gasps of the FrankenWagon, but they needed to keep moving quickly and without stopping.

It was also possible that Aprende would simply wait for them at the other end, but Neil was pretty sure he was hoping they just died of dehydration or starvation, or both, and then got picked apart by vultures.

So they walked and walked and walked.

"This is like the desert Guillermo had to survive to get to Pick-Me-Up," Larry said.

"You mean when he showed up half-dead?" The weight of Neil's backpack was starting to dig into his shoulder blades.

They had tried to hide in whatever shade they could find during the day, which wasn't much. Redheads and direct sunlight did not mix well. Despite ample applications of sunblock, he was sunburned.

Now it was night and cooling off fast. They were going to try to put as much distance between them and Aprende as they could before the sun came up.

"I'm hungry," Larry said.

"I can't risk a fire," Neil said. "We'd stick out like a lighthouse."

"I've got some of the cake Chef Hayes made for us back at the lodge," Larry said, pulling out the foil packet. "I ate some, but there's a bunch left. It's really good."

The lodge seemed like a year ago to Neil. So much had happened in just the past few hours, and he was tired.

"All right, hand some over."

Larry broke off a bit of the cake and handed it to Neil. Neil smelled the caramelized pineapple and peaches. They were perfectly cooked and had lost none of the flavor or freshness. He took a bite. The cake was crispy on the top and moist and flaky in the middle and sugary and sweet next to the fruit.

"How did he make this taste so good? It's so simple," Neil said.

"Anna gave you the recipe, remember?"

Neil took another bite. "I think I left it in the FrankenWagon. It didn't exactly seem to

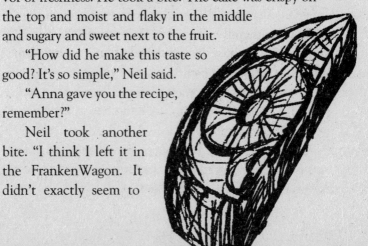

fit the 'necessary' bill when we were packing up."

"Now you'll never know the secret," Larry said.

Neil slid the rest of the cake into his mouth and chewed happily. He could feel life coming back into his body. That was what good food did. It didn't just give you energy—heck, a raw potato could achieve that much—but it excited all your senses. It inspired you. Chef Hayes's cake was doing that now.

"Let's move," Neil said.

"How much water you got left?" Larry asked.

Neil shook his canteen. It was almost empty. They'd made the mistake of drinking way too much when it was hot and dry. Now they were going to run low or run out.

"Not much."

"I've heard that you can last a couple of days without water . . . under normal circumstances. So we've got a whole day left."

"Thanks for the pep talk."

"Anytime. Well, at least anytime before tomorrow, when we die of dehydration."

"I have an idea." Neil stuck his nose in the air and smelled. Water didn't smell, but the minerals inside it did. Wet minerals had a different aroma than dry dust. It was worth a shot.

Neil smelled something better than water in just seconds. He smelled something sweet, with slight levels of sugar. "Larry, follow me."

Neil followed his nose and stopped in front of a weird-looking plant. The moonlight shone off large cactus pads. They looked like spiky Ping-Pong paddles with weird egg-shaped bulbs attached.

Neil pulled out his favorite knife (something he said was definitely a necessity) and hacked off a pad. Water trickled around the cut. "This was one of the edible bits Anna told me about in the canyon."

Neil held it up in the moonlight to get a better look.

Larry grabbed his hand. "Wait, I read some survival guides back home before we left."

"Really?"

"Jones lent them to me. This one book said that drinking water from a cactus is actually not good for you. There's acid and stuff in it."

"I can smell that," Neil said. "But there's fruit on this cactus that has a lot more than water inside. Read about the prickly pear?" He placed the pad on a rock and deftly skinned the fruit without sticking himself too much. He handed the watery inside to Larry.

His cousin gobbled it up greedily. "Not bad," he said. "Under the circumstances, excellent."

"Everyone thinks you need to drink to get enough water, but we get tons of water from veggies and fruits."

"And don't forget coffee," Larry said with a sigh. He'd emptied the last of his thermos hours before.

"The flesh of the pad also smells pretty good," Neil said. He skinned that as well and split it with his cousin.

"A desert feast!" Larry said. "There are no coffee cacti in the desert, are there?"

"No." Neil wiped his knife clean and put it back in

his pack. "Let's keep moving. If we come across anything else edible, I'll let you know."

Larry hoisted his duffel bag back on his shoulders. "The magazine did also suggest drinking our pee if we get really desperate."

"Yours might actually be caffeinated," Neil joked.

"You think so?" Larry said hopefully.

They hiked and hiked until the sun began to rise over the distant mountains.

"The sunrises and sunsets here are spectacular," Larry said, watching the golden ribbon light up the sky behind the peaks in an electric mix of pinks, blues, oranges, and yellows.

Neil stopped and looked. He took out his phone and snapped a picture. He began typing in Isabella's number to send it to her. But there was still no service. The power was low. He turned it off.

"Too bad we don't have a GPS out here." Neil shaded his eyes from the growing daylight. "We should find somewhere to catch some sleep, and keep out of sight."

"Good idea. Maybe there's a ranch house with steak and beans and beans!"

"I'll settle for anything with shade."

They looked around them. There were some rocky outcrops, and a few scrubby bushes, but almost everything was completely exposed.

"Should we go under those rocks?" Neil asked. "It looks cooler."

"I just saw a snake and a lizard scuttle under there to escape the heat, so any place we have to share with those will not work out well for us," Larry said.

Neil sat down on the ground and wiped his forehead. It was getting hot again.

Larry dropped his bag and unzipped it. "I have a better idea. Go get some sticks, and I'll get my raincoat."

Neil looked at the sky. There wasn't even one cloud. "Raincoat?"

"Just get the sticks. Long ones."

Neil walked around, the rising sun making the sticks seem to dance like snakes, but eventually he found three good long sticks. They were sanded almost smooth from years of exposure to the sun and wind.

He walked back to Larry, who was busy rubbing dirt all over his coat. "From up top it will look just like the ground all around us," Larry said. "Did you happen to pack any butcher's twine as a 'necessity'?"

Neil dug in his bag and handed a ball of heavy-duty string to Larry. "I figured as much," Larry said. "Go get some rocks and meet me over there." He pointed at the wind-blasted trunk of a long-dead tree a few yards away.

"Rocks will not be a problem," Neil said, looking around.

Larry carried everything over to the tree. He tied one corner of the coat to the trunk, then stuck the four branches in the ground about four feet apart, in a square.

The sticks didn't go very far into the hard ground, so Larry had Neil build rock piles around the base of each one.

Larry tied the other three corners of his coat to the sticks and stood back. It stayed upright, flapping slightly in the light breeze. Then he took some of his me-shirts and tied them together to make a curtain, blocking some of the rising sunlight.

"Voilà! Instant shelter." He took some more dirt and tossed it on the top of the raincoat to make sure it matched the desert floor.

Neil smiled. "We make a pretty good team."

"Now maybe we can actually get more than twenty minutes of sleep." Larry threw a towel on the ground, fluffed up his duffel bag as a pillow, and lay down. Within seconds he was fast asleep.

Neil had a little more trouble. He had too much running through his mind.

He could accept that Gravestone's ghost was really Aprende, but how had Aprende known to follow them to the Grand Canyon? How did he know they were looking for the mine? How did he know what clues Guillermo had told them to look for? Why was he working with this Whippet character to get the ranch from the Verdes?

And, just before Neil did succumb to exhaustion: How had Chef Hayes made such an amazing dessert?

CHAPTER TWENTY-ONE

HIS AND HERS

Neil awoke, the sunlight streaming into the shelter. He blinked. The sun was already heading down toward the mountains on the opposite side of the desert. He'd slept for hours and was hot and sweaty, but more refreshed than he had been in days.

The desert was quiet, beautiful in its way, and now that the sky was turning pastel shades and the air was cooling, it was even welcoming.

Neil's stomach rumbled.

"I know that sound!" Larry called. "Luckily, I've already opened a can of fish."

Neil walked over to the rock table Larry had set up. "Those aren't fish. They're three-hundred-dollar sardines from a small fishing village in Sicily."

Larry looked at the tin of shiny creatures. "They look like fish."

Neil reached in and grabbed one.

He held it under his nose and inhaled the briny aroma. Even here in the desert he felt transported to the shores of the Mediterranean Sea. He could almost hear the waves.

"Do you hear waves?" Larry asked. He stood up and scanned the horizon.

"It's just the wind," Neil said, happily savoring the sardines and wishing he'd packed a good crusty bread to go along with them.

"It is the wind," Larry said. "We'd better get moving." He began dismantling the tent while Neil ate his dinner. Neil even slurped the last of the oily juice in the tin, then wiped his mouth on his sleeve. "Survival never tasted so good," he said. He grabbed his backpack and then put the empty tin inside along with the can opener and some towels Larry had used. The backpack fell off the table and a white envelope fell onto the ground.

"Hey, I didn't leave that cake recipe behind after all," Neil said. He reached down to pick it up. The wind began to blow harder, and a gust took the envelope and sent it flying through the air.

Neil ran after it, the wind keeping it just out of reach. "You look like you're chasing a greased pigeon," Larry said, chuckling, as he stuffed the coat and shirts into his duffel bag.

The wind shifted abruptly and the envelope smacked Neil in the face. He grabbed it before it could sail away and then raised his hands triumphantly in the air. Then the wind changed again, swirling back, and Neil caught the smell of Aprende's gunpowder, getting stronger and closer by the second.

"Run!" he yelled. "He's here!"

Larry grabbed his duffel bag and Neil's backpack and they began running away as fast as they could. The wind was getting stronger and stronger and louder and louder.

"Maybe he's in a helicopter!" Neil said.

Larry tossed Neil his backpack. "Nope. This is Mother Nature. And it may be our only hope."

"What?"

"Just stay tuned and just keep running."

Neil didn't need more prodding.

The wind was now whipping up dust and tumbleweeds. Small pebbles dinged off their necks. It grew louder and Neil didn't hear the galloping hooves until the riders were almost on top of them.

They ran into a small gully, the remains of a long-dried creek bed. There was a rocky overhang, like a small cave, just to their left.

"Under there!" Larry called.

He and Neil nearly fell, stopping fast on the loose stones, but they were able to skitter over and duck under the rocks. Neil hoped Aprende hadn't spotted them and would just keep riding on. But Feleena had told them he was a great tracker, and she was right.

"Whoa!" Aprende yelled, and the horses stopped.

"Quick, get these on," Larry said, handing Neil a wet suit and scuba tank.

Neil didn't argue. He hurried to push his legs into the tight rubber.

The wind died down and they heard the clinking of spurs on the rock above them.

"I know you two are down there. I hope it's comfortable." It was the first time Neil had heard Aprende speak, and if he'd been told a ghost was speaking, he would have believed it. The voice sounded like it came from down a well, from someone who had eaten razor blades for breakfast. Hoarse and deep.

Neil slipped his arms into the wet suit, trying hard to keep his heart from bursting out of his chest.

"You two are supposed to be dead," Aprende said. "At least three times. I'm only here now because I expected to find your bodies on the desert floor, getting picked apart by buzzards."

Neil got one arm in, and crammed in the other. The tight suit was making it hard. He could hear the metal of Aprende's spurs scraping across the rock as he paced back and forth along the edge.

"What we have here, boys, is a failure to cooperate."

"Why don't you just shoot us," Larry yelled. "Get it over with."

"Don't put ideas in his head," Neil hissed.

"I figure he already had that one rattling around," Larry said.

"I could put a bullet into you both now," Aprende growled. "But that would lead to too many questions. I can answer them, but I prefer not to. Easier if you just get killed by

150

the desert. Every day some stupid city slicker goes and gets himself killed getting lost. No one asks questions in those situations other than, 'How stupid can two people get?'"

"We don't plan on letting you kill us now, any more than we let you kill us in the Grand Canyon," Larry yelled.

"Now, funny you mention the canyon," Aprende said, giving a low chuckle. "That old woman you shot before you escaped is one more reason folks won't shed no tears for a couple of cold-blooded killers found dead in the desert."

"What are you talking about?"

"Well, the body should turn up any day now. And the gun you used to shoot her, just after she led you out of the canyon, was found in that heap of junk you call a food truck." He gave another low cackle.

Neil and Larry were too shocked to speak. Neil clenched his fists so hard his fingers hurt. All Anna had done was try to help them, and now she was dead.

But Aprende wasn't done. "The more I ruminate on the situation, the more it seems that I *could* shoot you now. Tell folks I tracked you into the desert and you fired on me. What choice did I have but to fire back?" Neil heard the sound of Aprende clicking open his holster. Neil pulled his knife out of his backpack and got ready to fight for his life.

Just then they heard another rider approaching.

"Took you long enough," Aprende called out.

"I'm not as good a tracker as you, Joe," said another man. "Did you find 'em?"

"Hiding out like rats in a rat hole."

"So, what do we do?"

"I think you should talk to them, just so's they know why they got to die," Aprende said.

The man came to the edge of the rock and slung his feet over the edge, swinging his boots like a kid on a swing. Neil could have reached out and touched the heels.

"You two just had to get involved, didn't you?"

"We have no idea what you're talking about," Larry said. He and Neil scrunched up into the rock, sweltering now in their wet suits. The wind began to blow again.

The man laughed. "You fell for the Verdes' charm, and their insipid little ghost story. So they gave you the map and sent you out to help them. Did you ever wonder why they didn't go themselves?"

Neil and Larry looked at each other but said nothing.

"Because they know there's a curse over that mine, and anyone who gets close dies. You take all the risks, and they keep the gold, if you find it. Each year they dupe some idiot chef into doing their work for them. But my ancestor's ghost won't let anyone find it but a true heir."

"Your ancestor?" Neil couldn't help it. Despite the danger, he was curious.

"You know him as Gravestone Graves."

Larry scoffed. "Feleena said Graves died crazed and alone, with no family or anyone to mourn him." He was about to say that they'd even found Graves's body, but Neil grabbed his hand and put a finger to his lips.

The man gave a joyless chuckle. "That's because she and her father and every Verde before them are liars. Liars and cheats. Now, let me tell you the story that we tell around *our* campfires."

CHAPTER TWENTY-TWO

GRAVES'S SIDE

Major Ted Graves was a courageous man, an upright man. He helped to keep peace in a lawless land. The people respected him and nicknamed him Brave Graves. Part of his job was to make sure his men, whom he loved, were well fed.

A story came of a talented chef, Guillermo Verde, a man who could make wonderful meals out of the most meager of ingredients. If there was one staple of army food, it was meager ingredients.

Major Graves sought him out and asked him to join them on a survey of the surrounding mountains.

Verde said he would go, but he demanded double the wages of the other men. No, his greedy wife insisted, three times as much. Verde smiled and said Graves had no choice. He, Verde, had personally chased every other cook out of the town of Pick-Me-Up. It was give in to his demands, or try to feed the men himself.

This did not make Verde popular with the others, despite his skill with a fry pan, and they secretly wished him ill. But Graves knew the value of a well-fed group of soldiers, so he agreed, and he protected Verde from the others. What other choice did he have? It proved to be a fatal error.

As they trudged away from the town, a huge storm hit. Perhaps it was nature warning Graves that their mission was cursed, that he had invited a devil into his group. But Graves had a job to do, so he led the men on despite the raging winds and pounding rain.

Verde said he knew the area well and offered to act as a guide. He was hopeless. Soon they were lost. A giant lightning storm came up, with rain falling in sheets. There had never been such a cloudburst before or since.

"I know a secluded valley, an arroyo, where we can take shelter," Verde said, still pretending to know where they were.

Verde led them to a place where the wind and rain did indeed seem calmer. A small creek ran along the bottom, barely trickling. The men patted Verde on the back and walked to the creek to gather clean water to drink.

Even Gravestone seemed to think they had been saved . . . until a clap of thunder came rolling down the valley.

But it was not thunder. They looked up and saw a wall of white foam rushing toward them. A flash flood as high as the valley walls.

The men screamed and ran, and were swallowed up by the deluge.

Verde stood rooted to the spot, too yellow a coward to even move.

Graves knew their only chance was to cling to something solid. He grabbed Verde and, using his belt, quickly strapped himself and Verde together around the trunk of a tree. The wall of death smashed into them, pelting them with debris. For minutes it pounded, threatening to uproot the tree and carry them away. But just as Graves had all but given up hope of survival, the water began to recede. He gasped for breath as the river fell below his neck, then cheered as his feet once again touched ground. He untied the straps and gave a loud cheer.

He had saved their lives!

But Guillermo was not looking at Graves. He was examining something shiny on the ground. A nugget of gold as large as a man's hand lay at his feet. Verde picked it up, and Graves could see the fever grip his chef's heart and

soul. Greed. But Graves was not immune, sadly, despite his honorable heart. He thought of all the good he could do with a treasure. He could help the poor widows and children of the men who had died in the flood.

Together they walked back up the valley, finding more nuggets and flakes of gold. Halfway up the valley wall, they saw the source. The river had washed away a huge boulder, exposing a cave. Verde and Graves stepped inside. The walls were bare rock. Where had the gold come from? They heard a sound, like water draining from a tub, and they looked to the middle of the floor. Bits of gold hung suspended in a whirlpool of water, which was lowering quickly.

They waited until the hole was dry and then lowered a candle. The reflected light shone back at them like high noon. They had discovered a cave of wonders, with enough gold to fill a hundred kingdoms.

They worked for days to bring as much gold to the surface as they could.

"Neither one of us could have done all this alone," Graves said, examining the pile of gleaming treasure before them. "Half to each?"

"Indeed," Verde said with a snakelike grin. "By all means, fill your pockets, your hat, your saddlebags with as much heavy gold as you can carry."

Something in Verde's tone gave Graves pause, but he and Verde had toiled side by side for days. Surely they were partners.

No. Verde walked behind Graves as they went back into the rainy valley to begin their journey home. The valley still looked strange to Graves. He had never been here before. The river had begun rising again, more slowly this time, but still a strong current. Graves heard the sound of Verde behind him. He turned, but it was too late. Verde smashed his skillet down on Graves's head.

Graves fell into the swirling waters. The shock of the cold river woke him. He turned to see Verde grinning and laughing. "I'll see you in infierno!" Verde screamed.

Graves began to sink. The weight of all that gold dragged him to the bottom. He emptied his pockets as quickly as he could, but it was no use. He was washed under by the current and everything turned black. He should have died right then.

But fate had a different plan.

A large tree floated by, and a branch caught Graves's holster, lifting him out of the water. He floated for days, weeks, hours, who knows how long, before the river dried up.

He awoke, washed up on a dry desert gulch. No clues to determine where he was, nor where he had come from.

He walked and walked, hoping to stumble upon a town or army fort. The remaining gold became too heavy for his weary limbs to carry, and he had to throw it onto the desert floor.

After days and days of walking he stumbled on, of all places, Pick-Me-Up. The crowd, thinking him a homeless drifter, pelted him with garbage. He ignored them and walked up to the hotel, where Verde was holding court. Verde was surrounded by gold. His wife was giving away the finest champagne to anyone who would ask.

"You tried to kill me!" Graves screamed, rushing at Verde.

Verde calmly motioned for the sheriff to arrest the man. By now Verde had bribed everyone in town, and the sheriff did as he commanded.

Graves was shackled and thrown into a cold prison cell, where he was left to rot for an entire week.

Finally Verde paid a visit. He unlocked the cell door, gave Graves some water, and then said, "You can die here or you can run."

"Tell me where the mine is. Give me my half of the gold."

Verde smiled. "Never. My gold has been spent. I have purchased a wonderful ranch not far from here. I have no need of more."

"You are greedy. You will go back and I will follow you," Graves vowed.

Verde laughed a hollow laugh. "I will never return to the mine and will never tell anyone the location. It is better that it stay hidden than that it is found by a miserable wretch like you." He spat on him.

"Then why let me go?" Graves said, wiping the spit from his cheek.

"I can see that you have only a little time left. But hurry. The sheriff will return soon, and if he sees your cell open, he will shoot without asking questions."

Graves knew if he stayed he would die. He snuck away.

Days later he saw Verde's real plan. Wanted posters hung from every tree, saying the fugitive Ted Graves was armed and dangerous and should be shot on sight. There was a large reward, paid for by the new mayor of Pick-Me-Up, Guillermo Verde.

Graves's only chance to survive was to hide in the mountains—to live his life in the shadows, far from the reach of the Verde family.

But my ancestor did not give up his quest for the mine. For years he searched and searched. He met a woman in the mountains. Anastasia Whippet. They fell in love. She helped heal him and they raised a family. But still the injustice, the lure of the gold, drove him to keep searching.

One day he left, telling his wife he was sure that he had finally discovered the location of the mine. A secluded valley, he said, with a creek running on the bottom. And a large river close by, with cave dwellings. He left, even proudly wearing his tattered army uniform. He never came back.

Some believe he found the mine at last but was so exhausted he died on the spot.

Some say Verde followed him, killing him and leaving his body for the animals to eat.

Some say that his spirit guards the mine now, preventing anyone from touching that gold again. That the day it is found, the Graves family will rise again to reclaim what was stolen from them.

CHAPTER TWENTY-THREE

HABOOB

Whippet ended his story. The hot wind was howling. Despite this, even in the wet suit, Neil felt a chill. It wasn't just the ghost story, it was also a chill of doubt. The story was twisted, but believable. He could see how Graves and his descendants could feel wronged; even hate the Verdes.

If his story were true.

Whippet withdrew his legs and stood up. "And now that you have found the mine for us, we cannot risk you telling the Verdes the location. To do so would give them the victory my family has waited so patiently to achieve. Stealing their cattle, burning their barns, doing everything to bring them to the brink of ruin."

Larry turned to Neil. "They think we found the mine in the canyon!"

Neil yelled loud enough for Whippet and Aprende to hear.

"That wasn't the mine! It was a dead end, a fake!"

"Lying won't save you now," Whippet said. "The location fits the story exactly. You went down the hole. Joe here saw you. He watched as you lit the cave at the bottom. It 'lit up like the noonday sky,' he said. And he is not a man, I suspect you've noticed, given to poetic language."

"But it's not the mine! That was pyrite, not gold."

"Ha."

"Did you find any gold in the truck? Wouldn't we have taken some gold with us if we'd found some?"

Whippet and Aprende seemed to be involved in an animated discussion, but Neil couldn't hear it over the increasingly wild wind.

Finally Neil heard Aprende's spurs scrape their way to the edge. "Way we see it, you might be telling us the truth. But if you're lying, then the mine ain't going anywhere. And if you're telling the truth, the mine is still out there, and eliminating you two guarantees it stays hid until we can find it ourselves."

He fired a shot into the ground in front of their hideaway. "Now come out and we can get this over with quick."

Neil was shaking. There was nowhere to go.

"Keep stalling," Larry whispered. The wind was now almost hurricane-force, and Neil saw larger and larger branches skidding across the ground.

"But we can find it!" Neil said. "We can find the mine for you."

"I've been trailing you for days. You either did find it already, or you're so far off track that you never will."

"No! Verde was a chef. He may have been evil, but

he was a chef. You know from ransacking the truck that I'm a chef," said Neil.

"A great chef," Larry added.

"So what?" Aprende said.

"He left a recipe on the back of the map! It's got clues only a great chef could follow."

Aprende was quiet.

The wind howled.

"Get it over with!" Whippet yelled. "The sun'll be down soon, and I don't like the look of those clouds."

"I need to shoot them in the front, so everyone knows it was self-defense," Aprende said.

"Then jump down there and do it."

Larry got on his knees. "Get ready to run," he whispered.

Then, in a louder voice, "One of us has a gun. Anna gave it to us back in the canyon. You could come down here and shoot, but you better hit the one with the gun first or you're dead too."

Aprende gave a loud, long laugh. "Well, that clinches it. Now I know you're bluffing, and time's over for talkin'."

"On three," Larry whispered. Neil got into a runner's stance as Larry started counting down.

A gunshot rang out from up above.

"What the—" Aprende yelled. "Hector, get down!"

Another shot and Neil watched as Whippet toppled over in front of them, a crimson stain spreading across his pant leg. He stared at them, then got up and scurried away.

"Who in tarnation are you?" Aprende yelled.

Neil heard another voice, a man's voice. "You shot my best friend," he yelled. "She never came back. Her mule was all alone and covered in blood. I'm gonna make you pay!"

"Chef Hayes!" Neil said.

At that moment there was an exchange of gunfire and then a roaring like a train approaching.

"Now," Larry yelled. "And get that scuba mask on tight."

Neil ran.

He turned to look and his eyes grew wide. On the ledge, Aprende was hunkered down on the ground, firing his gun. Hayes was half-hidden behind a rock, peeking out from time to time and firing at Aprende.

Whippet had apparently found a safe spot to hide among the brambles and rocks. Except, Neil realized, there was no safe spot in the desert anymore.

Towering over everything was a scene straight out of a disaster movie. A giant yellow-brown wall of dust and sand. It was as high as ten skyscrapers and seemed to glow from inside. It looked, to Neil, like a tsunami made of Dijon mustard.

"What is that!?"

Larry lifted his mask for a second. "It's a haboob."

"A what?"

"It's Arabic for 'blowing.' It's a giant wall of dust that gets whipped up by the wind. Think of it as a thunderstorm with sand and dust instead of rain."

Neil didn't want to think about it at all. He zipped his wet suit up higher, despite the heat, and made sure his mask was on tight.

Everything became dark in a flash, and Neil was knocked to the ground by a powerful gust. Grit tore at his exposed skin as he struggled to get up and keep running. He could barely see Larry next to him. Larry's stupid scuba gear had now saved them three times.

Aprende's hat flew by Neil's head and sped off into the gloom. Tumbleweeds zoomed by as quickly as jet planes. Neil had seen the movie *The Wizard of Oz*. He mostly remembered the poor sanitary conditions of the pigs on the farm, but he also had a clear memory of Dorothy inside the twister, watching stuff spin by. This was a bit like that, except everything was heading in one direction.

Neil was thankful the wind was at their backs. Running into the wind would have been impossible.

Larry waved him to turn left, and they ran into a small gully. They scrambled among the rocks and weeds. After about ten minutes Neil was shocked to see green grass. Larry turned and smiled, the front of his mask scratched to bits by the flying debris.

He waved and they continued running, the ditch now overflowing with lush vegetation. They even passed a blue heron sitting in the bushes, with its head tucked into its wing to protect itself from the storm.

What was this place?

Neil took one more step and his sneaker landed in a puddle. A soaker! Water!

And then, even more odd than the heron, Neil saw a rowboat, and the rowboat was on the shore of a lake. A lake? Neil couldn't tell through the cloud if it was a thousand miles across, or ten feet.

Larry jumped into the rowboat and waved to Neil to follow him. Then they pushed off and began rowing out into the water.

As they sped away from the shore, the wind began to die down and the haboob began to dissipate. The sun 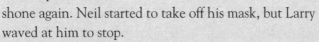 shone again. Neil started to take off his mask, but Larry waved at him to stop.

Larry continued rowing until they reached another shore. There was a rocky beach with picnic tables, and a nearby parking lot.

The dust had stopped swirling now, and Larry took off his mask. He was breathing heavily. "Ran out of oxygen about a minute ago." He gulped hungrily.

Neil took off his mask. "Why did you tell me to wait?"

Larry pointed at the receding storm. "The dust isn't just dangerous because it hurts. These storms whip up everything. Pollen spores, cat hair, animal feces. That storm is one big mass of germs and microbes."

"Gross."

Larry nodded, still taking deep breaths. "Yeah, and it can cause a thing called 'valley fever.' It's like the flu, and it shows up a few days or weeks later. My guess is that Aprende, Whippet, and sadly, Hayes are going to regret not packing scuba gear."

"Why didn't you tell me about all this when we were packing?"

"Hey, Neil," Larry said in his best fake-Larry voice,

"instead of your wok and favorite paella pan, I want to pack underwater gear so your nose doesn't get stuffed up in the desert." He looked at Neil.

"Okay. I might not have bought that then."

"Exactly. Now, I don't know about you, but I'm sweating like a pig in this getup, and a half-day jog through a dust storm didn't help. I'm going for a swim."

Larry began to strip off the wet suit. His T-shirt was soaked with sweat.

"What the heck is a lake doing out here in the middle of the desert?" Neil asked, unzipping.

"If I'm right, it's not a natural lake. I think it's Alamo Lake. It was formed when they built a dam. I think in 1968."

"Wow. Seriously? Your brain never ceases to amaze me," Neil said.

Larry gave an impish grin. "Not really." He pointed to a plaque next to the picnic table with the entire history. Then he slipped off the boat and into the water.

"Very shrewd," Neil said. He jumped in as well, and water had never felt cooler or cleaner in his life.

CHAPTER TWENTY-FOUR

CLEAN

Neil sat on the picnic table, letting the sun and air dry him off. The sun had almost set now. "We shouldn't stay here long. Aprende has already tracked us down plenty of times."

"That haboob covered our tracks pretty well," Larry said.

"Then we should at least figure out what we're doing next."

"True. Let me dance like a sick chicken first," Larry said, shaking the water out of his ear and looking very much like ill poultry as he hopped up and down on one foot.

"I wonder which legend is the right one." Neil was still shaken by the competing stories and what they said about the Verdes and the search for the mine.

Larry shook the dust out of his sneakers.

"As with most things, probably a little of both. Maybe Gravestone wasn't as horrible as the Verdes think, and maybe Guillermo did get greedy and refuse to help Graves. Maybe the Verdes aren't as peace-loving and giving as they look."

Neil thought about this. "But Salsa Verde is such an amazing place. You felt it too. I can't believe that Feleena and Julio could be cruel to anyone."

Larry nodded and dramatically placed his hands over his heart. "My inner Larry certainly tells me the same thing. But there's only one way to know for sure who's right."

"How?"

"Find the mine. If there's a skillet there with a bullet hole in it, we give everything to the Verdes so they can save their ranch."

"And if not? We give it to Whippet and Aprende?"

Larry snorted. "No way. Those jerks have tried to kill us three times. We keep it all ourselves and buy a new fleet of FrankenWagons."

Neil nodded. "Agreed. Although, can we buy something that looks less like recycled plane wreckage?"

Larry looked at him openmouthed. "I never thought you'd be the sort of person to judge a truck by its cover. Tsk-tsk. Poor Frankie. All this time you were just being judgey." Larry got up and stomped away indignantly.

"Oh, brother," Neil said. "Hey, I wonder if we get cell service here."

Larry sniffed and didn't answer.

Neil reached into his backpack. It was almost completely filled with sand and dust. "Oh no," he said. He dug and dug to find his phone, and pulled it out. The fine grit had completely gummed it up. He pushed the buttons over and over, but it refused to turn on.

"Great," he said. "Wrecked. Useless."

"It's probably for the best," Larry said. "Cops can track cell phones pretty easily. They use triangulation and radio tower frequencies to figure out where you're calling from."

"How do you know that?"

"TV," Larry said, smiling. "I'm not going to even turn mine on until we can get somewhere safe and a little less exposed."

"I'd like to talk to Angel or Isabella right now," Neil said, feeling even more remote and alone.

"Have you opened her letters yet?"

"I read the first one in the canyon. She didn't actually write anything on it. It was just a piece of paper, scented with her lavender perfume."

"That is so sweet I might go into a sugar coma," Larry said with a laugh.

Neil slugged him on the shoulder. "Maybe she wrote something on the second. But I've been saving it for next week."

"Open it. I think you need a little Tortellini Time right now. I'll leave you two alone and go see if there's a safe and secluded way out of here."

Larry walked toward the parking lot as Neil pulled out his backpack again. He reached in and took out an envelope. He sniffed. It smelled like cake. *Odd*, Neil thought. That wasn't one of Isabella's signature scents. He took a closer look. It was the envelope Anna had given them from Chef Hayes back at the Phantom Lodge.

Anna had helped them, saved them. And now she was dead. Aprende was horrible. Neil had no doubt that he would stop at nothing to kill the Flambés. He hung his head.

"Recipe or Isabella?" Neil said to himself. Even a few months before, the answer would have been recipe. Now? The cake recipe, as excellent as it was, could remain a secret for a few more minutes.

Neil stuffed it back in the pack and pulled out the right envelope. Isabella had written on this one: *Remember*.

He took out his knife and slit the envelope. A rush of flowery scent hit him like a spring day.

Somehow Isabella had figured out how to put on just enough scent that Neil's super-nose couldn't detect it through the envelope, but was a revelation when he cut the seal.

Her first scent had been lavender, the perfume she'd been wearing when they'd first met.

This was agave nectar based, a reference to the time they had spent in Mexico City. Neil closed his eyes and smiled, just remembering.

Larry came back and slung his duffel bag on his shoulder. "All right, lover boy, we should get a move on." He took the oxygen tanks and threw them into a garbage can. "Empty," he said.

"Like Aprende's soul," Neil said.

"You got that right. Anyway, I think I got us a good way to get out of here without being seen."

"Will I like it?"

"No," Larry said.

Larry and Neil walked into the parking lot. It was almost completely empty, except for one truck in a far corner. It was covered in dust.

"You want to steal a truck?" Neil said.

"I haven't done something like that in weeks," Larry said, pretending to be shocked. "No, this particular truck will be leaving here with its original driver in about thirty minutes."

"How can you be so sure?"

Larry pointed to a sign on the edge of the lot. PARKING LOT WILL BE CLOSED AND LOCKED ONE HOUR AFTER DUSK.

"I walked around. No tent or anything like that, so this truck is owned by someone here on a day trip, probably fishing, judging by the tackle box in the back and the hitch on the fender."

"Why didn't we see them on the lake?"

"They must have taken cover when they saw the haboob coming. We kept rowing and got here first."

As if on cue, Neil heard the humming of a motor coming from back toward the beach.

"So we're going to ask for a ride?"

"Don't be an idiot. You said it yourself that we're wanted criminals. We're going to hide in the bushes near the beach and wait until the owner gets the boat ready to hitch. They'll clean it and then put a tarp over the top. When they go back to get the truck, we'll sneak into the boat. It'll take them a good five minutes to clean the dust off, which should give us plenty of time to sneak inside."

"So why won't I like this plan? It seems great."

"They've been fishing all day. In the desert. And we'll be hiding under a hot tarp in a damp boat, with bait that's probably hours past its expiration date."

"Ugh," Neil said.

In fact, the smell wasn't nearly as bad as Neil had feared. The woman who owned the truck had caught a few fresh bass and stopped to clean them on the shore. The smell of fresh fish fillets was one Neil loved, and he forced his nose to focus on that, rather than how Larry or the bait smelled.

"So which way are we heading?" Neil asked. He didn't bother whispering. The truck and boat were rumbling noisily over the road.

"The sun set behind us just after we left the park, and I think we've been heading the same way the whole time. I'm betting we're heading for Phoenix."

Neil didn't know much about Phoenix. "It's the capital city, right?"

"YES! Somebody has been studying!" Larry beamed.

"Do you think the mine might be hidden there?"

"I highly doubt that. Phoenix has been booming for decades. There's hardly any of it that hasn't been dug up."

"So we're back at stage one. Argh." Neil leaned his head back and sighed heavily.

"The fruits thing was a good theory. It found us the fake mine, and Gravestone's body."

"The valley looked so close to the one on the map."

"Gravestone must have thought the same thing. Imagine how bummed he was when he got down the hole and realized it wasn't."

"Maybe he just convinced himself it was the right place, like we did. Sometimes when you want something to be true so much, you ignore the stuff that says you're wrong."

"Maybe the recipe isn't a clue at all," Larry said.

"It has to be. Guillermo had a whole recipe book full of pages, but he chose to draw the map on this one page. Why? There has to be something else. Why cake? Why fruits?"

"You're the chef in this team. What do you think?"

Neil was silent for a long time.

"I wonder what that cake recipe tasted like," Larry said, smacking his lips. "If this Guillermo was so talented, I bet it was awesome."

"It's hard to tell," Neil said. "It's so basic. He barely even mentioned amounts."

Larry continued smacking his lips. "Do we have any of Hayes's cake left?"

"I believe you vacuumed that up yesterday on the hike."

"Well, you did remember to bring the recipe, right?"

"It's in my backpack."

"Maybe you could make some more! I'll bet it will be *almost* as good."

It was dark, but Neil heard the sarcasm in Larry's voice. "Yeah. Almost. It was good, though. Anna said it was just like the cake her grandfather had. . . ."

Neil sat up straight. "How old was Anna?"

"She said she was seventy-something, but I think she was shaving some decades."

"So her grandfather would have been around, easily, a hundred years ago."

"I guess so. She might have been too. Why?"

"Do you have a light?"

"I've got one on my phone," Larry said. "But if the truck begins to slow down or you hear any other traffic on the road, shut it off. We don't need anyone looking under this tarp until we're out of here."

Larry handed Neil the phone. He flicked on the flashlight and rummaged in his pack for the recipe.

His fingers were trembling as he opened the envelope. Chef Hayes had written down precise instructions for "Chuck Wagon Skillet Cake." The ingredients were exactly the same as the recipe on the back of the map.

The one big difference in the recipe in Neil's hands was that Chef Hayes had also included the method for cooking it properly.

"I'm such an idiot," Neil said.

"Agreed. Why?"

"I knew as soon as I tasted that cake exactly how it was made. How Hayes kept the fruits so perfectly moist and yet fully cooked."

"And?"

Neil held the page up to Larry and pointed. Under the recipe was a picture of the proper way to get a skillet cake out of the pan and onto a plate.

The skillet was flipped so that the cake came out on a plate, with the fruit on top.

"It's the recipe for upside-down cake!" Larry's face broke into a grin.

"The map is supposed to be read upside down. We're not looking for a valley. We're looking for a mountain."

Just then the truck slammed to a stop and sirens began to wail.

CHAPTER TWENTY-FIVE

FISHING

"We've got to get out of here," Neil said, his heart racing. "They tracked us!"

"Shhhhh," Larry said, putting a hand on Neil's shoulder to calm him. "We don't know that. Maybe this is just a roadblock or a traffic accident."

They heard Aprende's voice. "Ma'am, we have reason to believe that you are harboring two fugitives from the law in your vehicle."

"That's insane!" said the woman. "I am a judge!"

"You don't mind if we take a look around, do you?" Aprende said.

"You got a warrant?" said the woman. They heard her open her door.

Aprende chuckled. "Just a quick peek, ma'am. Let's keep this friendly-like." There was a decidedly unfriendly tone of menace in his voice.

"How did he find us?" Neil whispered.

"That guy is one heck of a tracker. Or he's a ghost," Larry said.

"He's going to find us in here. He's going to kill us."

"He can't shoot us in front of all these cops," Larry said.

"I wouldn't put anything past him," Neil said, shuddering.

Aprende's spurs jingled on the road as he circled the truck. The sound was barely audible over the engines of the cars and the chatting officers.

The woman followed, arguing with Aprende that he had no right to search her private property.

"Do you know who I am? I could have your badge. If I'm late for the gala tonight, I *will* have your badge!"

Neil's mind was racing. It was impossible. How could Aprende have tracked them across so much territory, during everything from the dead of night to the dead middle of a giant dust storm?

What had Neil and Larry had with them the entire time? The scuba gear? They'd left the tanks back in the park. Everything else had been left in the FrankenWagon . . . except . . . Neil felt the straps on his shoulders.

"It's my backpack," Neil said. "That's how he's been able to track us. That's how he found us in the cave. It's how he found us in the desert. Somebody put a homing device in the backpack."

"This is good news!" Larry said.

"How?"

"I've got an escape plan."

"How do we get out of here with all those cops surrounding us?"

"That's the genius. We don't have to."

Larry took the cookbook out of the backpack. He ripped out a page and hastily scribbled a note.

Found out how you're such a great tracker.
Good luck tracking us now, you possum-butt-kissing slacker!

Larry had added a smirking possum face, for good measure. Then he pinned the note to the backpack and strapped it onto one of the seats.

"Not my best work. You'd think after chasing Shakespeare for the past few weeks I'd be a better poet."

"That's your plan? Won't he notice we actually *are* still here? Or do you think he'll read the note and be so offended he'll walk away?"

Larry responded by reaching down and grabbing a ring that was set in the floor of the boat. "This is the deluxe model of the Primestar 5000 coastal-range fishing vessel. That's how I knew the owner was going to put a tarp on top. Very pricey boat. I've been on one of these before with Gary."

"So?" Neil was completely confused. Gary had been one of his sous-chefs when he still had Chez Flambé.

"Gary's uncle uses one when he sport fishes. It's got everything, including a toilet and a holding tank for the sewage."

Larry quietly turned the latch. Neil was assaulted with the overwhelming smell of old bathroom, dead fish, and algae.

"And there's room for two."

"You're kidding!" Neil gagged.

"You can stay here and try your luck with Sheriff Possum Puss, then."

The jangle of Aprende's spurs grew louder.

"Argh," Neil said.

"It'll take him a few minutes to open that tarp. Get in."

Neil held his nose as tightly as possible as he slipped into the smelly mass of lake water and . . . he didn't want to think about what else was in there with them.

Neil could hear the snaps on the tarp being undone.

Larry tucked himself in beside Neil and slowly lowered the hatch.

"This stinks," Neil hissed.

"Don't make me laugh. The last thing I want to do is swallow any of this stuff!"

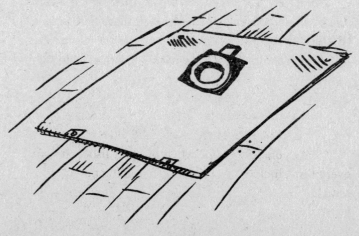

The door muffled most of the noise, but they could hear Aprende chuckle as he saw the backpack. "Well, well. Isn't this proof that—" Then he stopped as he read the note. He gave an angry yell and slammed the side of the boat with either his fist or his boot.

Neil did his best not to gasp, at the same time trying not to throw up.

"There," said the woman. "That's as far as you go. There's nobody in here but some fresh bass. And if they don't get into my refrigerator soon, they're going to go bad. And the governor, my *good friend* the governor, is expecting some fresh fillets at our dinner tonight. Understand?"

Aprende slammed the tarp back down.

There were more muffled noises as the cops cars sped off.

The truck lurched back onto the road, sending the wastewater in the holding tank sloshing into Neil's face.

"ACK! Can we get out of here now?" Neil said, fighting a losing battle against the stench.

"Not yet," Larry said. "What if Aprende left a camera or a microphone or something in there, just in case? Better safe than sorry."

"I don't think I could be more sorry than I am right now."

CHAPTER TWENTY-SIX

RISING IN PHOENIX

The ride to Phoenix was uneventful, if revolting. The woman parked the truck. They didn't hear a garage door open or close, so they assumed it was in a driveway. They heard the truck door open and the woman muttering loudly about Aprende and how she was going to make him pay.

"She must be somebody important," Neil said.

"She's definitely scary. Standing up to Aprende like that."

The tarp snapped and the woman rummaged inside, grabbing the icebox with the fish fillets. She was still swearing angrily as she marched away. They heard a screen door slam and then her voice disappeared.

"Time to go," Larry said. "If she does have a party

tonight, she's going to take a while to clean up and dress."

"Thank goodness!" Neil said, practically leaping out of the hatch door and taking huge breaths of the relatively fresher air. His backpack was gone. "Thank goodness I grabbed the map," he said.

They peered out from under the tarp. It was dark. A crescent moon was just beginning to rise on the horizon.

"Coast is clear," Larry said. He grabbed his duffel bag and they slipped over the edge of the boat.

Neil followed after him, leaving a smear of waste down the side.

"Should we clean that?" he asked. "She'll know Aprende was right about us being stowaways."

"We don't have time. Anyway, I'm willing to bet she's so ticked at the guy there's no way she'll call him."

"So, where to now?"

Larry shrugged. "We've got to find someplace to get some fresh clothes, maybe a shower."

"Maybe?"

Larry just grinned and motioned for Neil to follow

him. They slipped among huge flowering azaleas along the side of a residential street. Dozens of identical stucco houses lined both sides.

"Must be getting late," Neil said.

"I'll bet it's around nine," Larry said, looking up at the moon and stars. "Or close to it."

They kept to the shadows and bushes, all the time listening for the sound of a siren or jangling spurs.

"So, the map is upside down," Larry said as they hid behind a large bush while a car passed by.

"Hayes's cake is an upside-down cake. That's how you top it with fruit, or fruits. You put them on the bottom, and when it's done and you flip the skillet over, the fruits are cooked on the bottom but end up on top."

"So all these years everyone, including Gravestone and the Verdes, have been looking for a valley."

"When Guillermo was telling them the cave is in a mountain."

Larry chuckled, shaking his head. "You chefs are a sneaky bunch. So where do we start?"

"I'd suggest going back to the Verdes and asking them if there are any mountains close by that look like the mountains on the map."

"There's an implied *but* in that sentence."

"My heart tells me that Feleena and Julio are honest and trustworthy, but that tale Whippet told us still has me shaken."

"I get it. And I'm willing to bet Feleena *wasn't* lying when she said Aprende left armed snipers hidden around the ranch in case we came back."

The car passed and they continued their walk.

"Phoenix doesn't exactly seem like a booming city," Neil said as they passed more and more streets with big houses. "Where are the skyscrapers?"

"This must be Scottsdale," Larry said. "It's the rich northeast of the city. Lots of golf courses and mansions. It's also close to a big mountain, where I think we'll have our best chance to sneak away."

Neil groaned. The adrenaline that had kept him going was now gone, and his legs felt like rubber.

"How far is this mountain?"

Larry pointed straight ahead, and Neil saw a large shadow against the backdrop of the stars.

"Not far. The most expensive homes are all close to the mountains here. You get a great view, easy access to the parks. It's perfect, except for the occasional scorpion."

Neil stopped. "The occasional what?"

"Scorpion. Don't worry. Almost no one actually dies from a scorpion bite. Just make sure you check your shoes before you put them on in the morning. They love hiding there at night. Now, let's get moving."

Neil made a mental note to never take off his shoes in Arizona again.

They jumped a wall, crossed a couple of roads, and finally reached the base of the mountain.

Neil looked around for any sign of scorpions as Larry quickly scrambled up the rocky slope. Neil jumped with fright more than a few times as they passed more saguaro cacti and mesquite bushes. After about an hour, he'd had enough. Neil sat down on a rock.

"Larry. I can't go any farther. I'm totally bagged. Is there any way we can set up a tent or at least grab a nap here?"

Larry looked all around. The lights from Scottsdale were still bright and close. "We're too exposed. Just give me ten more minutes. I see something up ahead that looks promising. It might be a shelter." He ran ahead.

The temperature had been dropping, and Neil shook with the cold. He stood up and forced himself to move. At least it was warmer than sitting still. After a few minutes he heard Larry's voice coming from somewhere up ahead.

"You've got to see this!"

Neil walked around a cluster of trees and cacti and blinked. The moonlight was reflecting off a bizarre circular mixture of sheet metal, wood, and glass. It was about fifteen feet high and resembled a giant dented soup can, with windows.

"What the heck is this?" Neil said, walking slowly toward the structure, not completely convinced he wasn't hallucinating. "Is it abandoned?"

Larry stuck his head out of a top window. "You won't believe what this place has inside!" he said. "Bunk beds and a woodstove! I'll light a fire." Larry disappeared back inside.

Neil could smell coconut from nearby. He sniffed. Not real coconut, but the oil that got used in soaps and shampoos. He looked to his right and saw a wooden shack with a large metal barrel on top. A shower? He'd seen something similar on the beaches back home.

Neil smelled like a sewer. He'd sleep better if he had a shower. Despite his exhaustion, he walked into the shower and felt around, hoping like heck that scorpions didn't also like the smell of peach and apple foam bath soap.

As he groped in the darkness, he pulled on a rope, and before he could even consider taking off his clothes, he was hit with a rush of lukewarm water.

"Yes!" he said. He grabbed the soap and began scrubbing his clothes as well as every inch of his smelly self. He threw the clothes, piece by piece, over the edge of the stall to dry, then walked out of the shower refreshed, cleaned, and practically naked except for his soaking-wet shoes.

He squeaked a few steps toward the soup can, shivering but happy.

"Well, that's a funny-looking bathing suit," said a woman's voice.

A young woman in jeans and a leather jacket stood in the moonlight, arms on hips.

"Now, who are you and why are you messing up my homework?"

CHAPTER TWENTY-SEVEN

HOMEWORK

Larry sat on a stool by the glowing stove, happily slurping from a fresh mug of coffee. "This place is your homework?"

Selma Kubrick nodded and refilled his mug.

"I'm studying at the architectural school. It's up the mountain a ways."

"There's an architecture school on a mountain?"

Selma nodded. "Yup. Each year they pick only the top students from around the country. They send us out here into the wilderness, or at least as close as we get to wilderness this close to Phoenix, and we have to build our very own survival shelter. It has to be cheap, made with recycled materials, but livable, with as many amenities as you can cram inside. I think this one's gonna land me an A-plus."

"It is totally cool!" Larry said. "I love the way you have everything tucked away when you're not using it."

He turned to Neil. "I checked it out while you were having your little skinny-dip."

Neil blushed as he wrapped the wool blanket Selma had loaned him even tighter around himself.

Selma smiled. "I am pretty proud. The stove folds into the wall when you're not using it. The beds collapse into the floor. The bathroom is outside, as you saw, but I'm thinking of different ways to incorporate that inside as well."

"You should design an enviro-friendly food truck!" Larry said.

"Well, the earth isn't getting any bigger, and we need to stop wasting so much stuff. Look down there at those giant houses." She indicated the glowing lights of the city. "This shelter I built could happily house a young couple. Down there they've got ten rooms they don't even use more than a day a year. Those rooms are heated in the winter, cooled in the summer. It's crazy."

"Downsizing," Neil said. "You think we need to downsize."

"Exactly! Using only what we need and not what we want."

Neil thought about that. "Larry mentioned the food truck. We've been downsizing as well."

"You're a chef?" Selma said. "Cool. How much meat do you cook?"

"Um, right now, none. But it's usually on the menu every day."

"Total waste," she said. "Meat is killing the environment, taking up land, food. Once a week is more than enough."

Isabella had said something similar to Neil on more than one occasion. His cell phone was still busted, but he desperately wanted to call her. Or Angel, or Sean Nakamura, or even his parents.

"I've been thinking about cutting back," was all Neil said.

"Good. So what brings you two climbing up a mountain in the middle of the night? You running from the cops?"

Neil and Larry looked at each other.

"I'll take that as a yes. Why?"

"It's complicated," Neil said. "And I'll understand if you don't want us around after I tell you. But please, don't call the cops."

Selma seemed to inch back toward the front door.

"I reserve the right to react in whatever way I please."

"Fair enough. First off, we are not dangerous."

"Just dangerously handsome!" Larry said.

"You can probably tell that's not true just by looking at us."

Neil told Selma about the Verdes, the mine, and also their flight from Aprende and his posse.

"Hmmm," she said, rubbing her chin for a few seconds. "The food poisoning story sounds kind of familiar. Maybe even the food truck thing. I can't recall any pictures of you two on the TV, though. And I certainly haven't heard any news stories about anyone getting shot in the canyon."

"You think Aprende made that up?" Neil asked, looking at Larry.

Larry shrugged. "Let's hope."

The thought that Anna might still be alive made Neil feel better.

"So, that's our story. We're trying to help someone save their ranch, avoid getting thrown in jail, or killed, for crimes we didn't commit."

Selma threw back her head and laughed. "You'd have to be an idiot to make up something like that! I believe you," she said, slapping her knee.

"Did you actually just slap your knee?" Larry said.

Selma stared at him, her eyes narrowing. "You making fun of me?"

Larry beamed. "Not in the least!"

Neil decided to step in and end the banter. "Selma, can we stay here just one night? I haven't had more than a few minutes' sleep in days. And we'll be gone tomorrow, promise."

Selma thought for a while. "Look. Here's the deal. I think you're innocent, but I also don't need any nutso cops coming in and getting me in trouble with the school. So I'm taking a big risk if I let you stay."

Neil got up to leave. His sneakers squeaked. He hoped his pants were dry. "Thanks anyway."

Selma waved her hands to sit him back down. "Hold on! That's not what I'm saying. You can stay one night. *But*, I want some of this gold, if you find it."

"It's not really ours to give out," Neil said.

Selma smiled. "If you find that skillet, it's all yours. That's the law."

Neil thought about this.

"I don't want a lot. Just enough to pay my school debts and maybe set me up with an office where I can actually sell my stuff to other people."

Larry and Neil looked at each other and nodded. "Here's what we can promise," Larry said. "I will ask Feleena and Julio. I'm sure that if they're as kind as they seem, they won't balk at sharing."

Selma held out her hand. "Deal?"

Larry took it. "Deal."

She helped them set up the beds, showed Larry where to hang the coffeepot when he was done with it, and then closed the door.

A soft rain began to fall, tinging off the metal roof. It made different sounds as it hit different parts of the building, creating a kind of lullaby music.

"That woman is a genius," Neil said as he began to sink into his pillow.

Larry snorted. "Not about everything."

"Waddyoumean," Neil mumbled.

"She thought I'd be done with the coffeepot!"

Selma knocked lightly on the door and Neil opened his eyes. Light was streaming in. The rain had stopped. She opened the door a crack and Neil was inundated with the oddest scent he'd ever encountered. It was like molasses combined with decaying leaves and freshly mowed grass.

"What's that smell?" he said, rubbing his eyes.

"Creosote. It's one of the coolest things about the desert. The creosote bushes hold on to it until it rains, and then it just kind of explodes into the air. We call it the smell of spring around here."

"What time is it?"

"About noon, actually."

"Why isn't this place boiling?" Neil asked.

Selma smiled. "The roof pools the cool water, and as

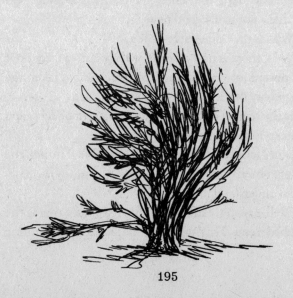

it evaporates, it carries the heat away. Also, you'll notice the windows are at the top of the shelter. Hot air rises and escapes, pulling the cooler air in from the ground."

"Amazing. You do need to design our next food truck."

"When I set up my office, you'll be my first customers. That is, if the sheepdog up there ever wakes up."

Larry was snoozing away, hugging the empty coffeepot like a teddy bear.

"Pathetic," Neil said.

"I slept at the main school last night, and I did a little checking on your story."

"And?"

"Good news and lots of bad news."

Neil swung his feet over the side of the bed, the blanket still wrapped around him.

"Give me the good news."

"There's not much. There's still no story about a shooting in the canyon. But they did find a donkey wandering alone along the trails. The owner is missing. So I guess that's not really good news."

"What's the undeniably bad news?"

"Well, there is now a poster with your two faces on it and a reward for your capture. So Aprende has taken the chase public. But it's not front-page news yet."

"Is the reward enough to cover your school debts and set you up in business?"

Selma looked at the ground. "Yes. But I'm not the type to go back on my word."

"I'd understand if you did."

"Well, I won't. And part of the reason for that is the other bad news. This Whippet character isn't planning to build houses on the site of that ranch you were talking about."

"Salsa Verde."

"He's planning to raze the whole thing flat, including the hills and some of the valley, and then build a giant open-pit mine."

Neil was aghast. The thought of all that beauty being ripped up and then carted away by giant trucks and bulldozers shocked him.

"How do you know?" he said.

"One of the advantages of being enrolled at the school is that we have access to the urban planning databases for the state."

Larry sat up in bed. "Maybe he thinks the gold mine is on the property?"

"You've been listening the whole time?" Neil asked.

"Hole time! That's funny, because you're talking about a hole in the ground."

Neil and Selma didn't laugh.

"It started off as you guys talking in my dream. Neil was a giant rabbit and you were a coyote in a wig. Very weird. Anyway, back to my question. You think Whippet thinks the lost mine is there?"

Selma shrugged. "The application says he thinks there's copper and uranium. His company goes all over the world doing stuff like this. I studied that ranch house in school. It's one of the best examples of how to combine old and new ideas, and do it well. Anyone who'd just rip it down like that is no friend of mine."

They all sat in silence for a few minutes. Selma eventually got up and set up the stove. She put on the kettle for more coffee and then prepped the batter for some griddle cakes.

"Pull back on the baking powder a touch," Neil said, sniffing the air. "They'll get too fluffy and won't cook all the way through."

"Um, okay," Selma said. "Go get your clothes back on and I'll start cooking."

"And start making more coffee?" Larry asked eagerly.

"Of course."

Breakfast was excellent, and Neil felt the strength returning to his legs.

Larry's coffee imbibing also raised his energy level to higher than recent levels.

"Before we go, can I get you to do me a favor?" Neil asked.

"What?"

Neil handed Selma an envelope. "Mail this to my friend Isabella." He had taken some leaves from a nearby creosote bush and folded them inside the paper from her last note.

Selma nodded. "I'll fire it off later today when I go into town."

Neil and Larry had decided to head back to Pick-Me-Up. They were now looking for a mountain, and figured starting from Guillermo's first footsteps was still the best plan. Of course, there were a lot of people and city between them and the ghost town.

Larry slapped Neil on the back. "Time for us to mosey on down the trail, Slappy. Time's a-wastin'."

Neil sighed but Selma chuckled. "The best way to get out of here unseen is to stick to the side of the mountain and head west until Scottsdale ends, then switch south through the suburbs. You'll eventually hit the Salt River."

"Sounds delicious!" Larry said.

"Well, it'll at least have some water in it after the rain we had last night. You can either follow it into the city, which I don't recommend if you want to lie low, or cross it and continue through Mesa and down into the mountains south of the city."

"Won't we look suspicious walking through all those neighborhoods?" Neil asked.

"Who said anything about walking?"

"Are we driving?"

"Nope. But there are two mountain bikes, with helmets, stashed behind the shelter two over. One of the former students left them behind a couple of years back, and we use 'em for trips from time to time. The helmets are those big full-head ones. Hot, but they should keep you from being recognized. But stick to the side roads once you hit Mesa."

"You are awesome!" Larry leaped over and gave her a huge hug.

"Thanks. Just make sure you return them."

Larry pressed his hands to his heart. "As Slappy here is my witness, I shall deliver your gentle steeds unharmed and unhurt."

"And, we hope, laden with gold."

CHAPTER TWENTY-EIGHT

CYCLE PATHS

I'd like to try calling someone from your phone," Neil said.

"Nope. Not a good idea." Larry didn't bother to lower the binoculars he'd "borrowed" from the shelter with the bikes. He and Neil were sitting on the top of the mountain, overlooking the descent into Mesa.

The bikes had proven to be the perfect way to scramble across the mountain quickly and relatively quietly.

But Neil was back to being exhausted, and he wanted to call in some help from his friends. "What about a text message?"

"Look at the top of each mountain around the city."

Neil looked from peak to peak. Hundreds of antennae

and cell towers glimmered in the fading sunlight. "So?"

"You know how, when you make a phone call on the road, the cell company instantly knows you're roaming?"

"Yeah. I've had arguments with my parents about the bills after almost every one of our trips."

"Exactly. Turn on my phone here, and if Aprende is listening, there are enough cell towers around to almost perfectly pinpoint where our phone signal is coming from."

"Why do more towers make that easy?"

"If you call, and there's only one tower, you could be anywhere in a giant circle stretching out from that tower. They can use GPS on the phones, but that takes longer. But if the call is rebounding off a bunch of towers, then they can figure out how far you are from each one. Plot that on a map and in ten seconds we'll be overrun with cops."

Neil kicked a stone. It flipped down the side of the mountain, sending a roadrunner scurrying for cover. All the good feelings he'd had at Salsa Verde were leaking away like the filling from a poorly cooked blintz.

"Maybe we could just head back home?"

Larry put down the binoculars. "I'm missing home too. I wish we could contact everyone and let them know what's going on. But with this nutbar after us, it's just not worth the risk."

"I just want this to be over. It started off kind of fun, but it's turned into a nightmare."

The sun began setting behind the western mountains,

sending pink and yellow streaks far into the sky.

"Time to go," Larry said. "We'll go slowly but steadily and we should be able to cycle through most of the busy streets by dawn."

Neil sighed. Another night without sleep. He strapped on his helmet. He and Larry began bombing down the mountain toward the suburbs.

The setting sun shone off the rocks, giving them a pinkish glow. They reached the bottom quickly and then saw the shining golden ribbon of water a few miles in the distance.

"That must be the river. Let's head there and we'll follow the shore until we can cross."

Crossing didn't take too long. They quickly found a bridge and then pedaled as fast as they could, south. They passed under numerous highways and overpasses and mall after mall.

Neil pulled up alongside Larry and flipped open his visor. "This is a bit weird. I haven't seen one pedestrian the whole trip."

"Arizona seems to be a car state. Not bad for bikes, either, but everything is just so far apart, and this is really the western suburbs, not the downtown."

The streets did seem to stretch on forever. Neil had grown up in Vancouver, a small city with mountains and the ocean on three sides. That kept everything mostly crammed together. He'd visited suburbs, but the whole city of Phoenix seemed to be one big suburb.

"I see what Selma meant about taking up space," Larry said.

Neil nodded and closed his visor. He still wanted to

get back to wilderness as quickly as possible.

Apart from the occasional police car siren in the distance that gave them a scare, they passed through the Phoenix suburbs unnoticed. The last rays of the sun disappeared as they approached a giant shadow on the horizon.

Larry rode up next to Neil. "Not much light to go by up ahead."

"What's the deal?"

"Selma was telling me about it. The land south of there is owned by different native groups. The city built right up until the very edge and then, boom, stopped."

Neil pedaled as the darkness grew closer. "So what do we do?"

"It's actually a good place to hide. We cycle in as far as we can and then find a place to sleep without being seen."

The road they were on didn't stop when the lights stopped, and they continued cycling into the growing night. They flicked on their headlights, but only Larry's seemed to have fresh batteries. He and Neil cycled close together, trying to use the dim glow to keep them from skidding off the road or hitting a rock that had been left in the middle.

The stars began coming out one by one, and soon the sky was filled with millions of twinkling lights.

"Wow," Neil whispered.

"That's another advantage of the desert," Larry said. "There's hardly any moisture in the air, so the light passes through unfiltered. That's science."

Neil could tell that the road was rising underneath

them, and his legs began to burn with the effort of a full day of cycling.

Larry slowed down. Car headlights approached from far away. "Time to get off this road. Let's find someplace to sleep."

"Agreed. But no scorpions."

"No promises." Larry laughed and led them off into the bush. The terrain was bumpy, but Neil was happy when he heard the car drive by and couldn't see its headlights.

"I see some bigger rocks up ahead," Larry said. "With a cave."

Neil could see them too. It was amazing how bright the night sky could be, even without streetlights. He could also smell the faint aroma of charred wood, burnt marshmallow, and stale pop. The remains, he was sure, of an impromptu weekend party.

"I don't think we're the first ones to camp out here."

"That's good. It means it's probably a dry cave. No scorpions."

Neil breathed a sigh of relief.

"Of course, I make no promises about rattlesnakes."

"You're kidding, right?"

Larry just chuckled and skidded to a stop by the cave. He shone his bike light around and even kicked the remains of the campfire to see if anything was hiding.

"Coast is clear, chicken," he said. He laid down his bike

and then unzipped his duffel bag. Selma had loaned them a couple of blankets, and Larry spread them on the ground. "A fire might be a good idea," he said.

"Think we can risk a small one?" Neil rested his bike against the mouth of the overhang. "It is getting chilly. And I'm starving."

"We can warm up some of the canned refried beans Selma gave us."

"Delicious," Neil said. He didn't mean it, but he volunteered to find wood, and soon returned. He set about lighting a small fire and prepping dinner. "I would kill for some fresh poblano chiles," he said, stirring the beans in the can. "Even some aged Manchego cheese would save this meal."

"Don't be so picky," Larry said, stretching out on his blanket and watching the smoke from the fire curl and wisp along the ceiling of the cave.

"Says the guy who demands elephant poop coffee whenever we go out."

"I don't expect it when I'm on the run in the desert," Larry said. "Although any coffee would be good right now."

"How do you avoid waking up with splitting caffeine-withdrawal headaches?"

"With you around, I'm never sure what causes my headaches."

"Ha-ha. So, we've passed through the city. Now what?"

"Aprende can't track us now, at least not using whatever he hid in the backpack. So we need to keep searching for this mountain on the map and not get caught."

"Thanks. I figured that part out on my own. I mean how do we actually find this mountain?"

"Well, we were on the right track the first time. Look for a place that is close to some cave dwellings and has some water running nearby."

"We never did figure out the trees thing."

"Yeah, that is a bit of a mystery. And do you think the fruit thing was a misdirection?"

Neil rubbed his upper lip. "For the mine, yes. But it was a clue a chef left for a chef to find. I think that's what Guillermo meant by only a Verde with 'great skill.' He meant the skill you needed to recognize the real clue, the skillet cake recipe."

"So, really, Chef Hayes is the hero of this story."

Neil was about to get mad, argue that only he was a great chef, that he had made the connection between the cake and the recipe. But he stopped himself. "Yes. Hayes is a great chef. And if he hadn't been there in the desert, we'd likely be dead."

Larry looked at him, surprised. "New Neil makes a comeback! I was expecting you to dislodge some rocks at the mere suggestion that someone was better than you."

"I should have figured the secret out sooner. And I might never have if he hadn't given me the recipe." Neil used a rag to lift the beans from the fire and put the tin on the ground between them. They gathered around the tin, and Larry pulled two spoons from his duffel bag.

"These beans are excellent," Larry said, stuffing a spoonful into his mouth. "But there's more than beans in this. What did you do?"

Neil smiled. "I took a walk and collected some

plants. Nothing poisonous, I think."

Larry stopped chewing. "You're kidding, right?"

"Were you kidding about the rattlesnakes?"

"Touché," Larry said, chewing again. "But what did you find?"

"Just some fruit buds off some trees and a few cactus flowers."

Larry wolfed down another spoonful. "Chef Hayes may know how to make a skillet cake, but you my redheaded friend, are a true genius."

Neil gave a slight nod. The sparks from the fire circled above his head. Outside some birds flew past. It was otherwise completely silent. He started to nod off.

Larry was now running his finger inside the hot tin, gathering up the last of the beans and sauce. Neil snuggled close to the fire and wrapped himself in his blanket.

"So tomorrow we start looking for a mountain that fits the bill, and then head south to Pick-Me-Up?"

"That's the plan," Larry said, licking his fingers. "You know, that Guillermo was a funny guy."

"How?" Neil said, already dozing and dreaming of flying like a bird over the Arizona desert and back home.

"Well, the whole map is a visual pun. And then he throws those trees in just to mess with us."

"Mess with us?"

"The trees made sense when we were headed up

north. Lots of pine and stuff. But the farther south we head, the drier it gets. Good luck finding that many trees together now."

"Uh-huh," Neil said, his eyes closed. A bat flew past the cave opening, chirping.

Neil's eyes flew open. "Larry. We've got to get back to the ranch, and we've got to see it from the air."

CHAPTER TWENTY-NINE

SHOPPING

Neil, I'm telling you, I don't know how to fly a plane."
Larry shook his head and continued to pack his duffel bag.

Neil rubbed his temples. "The one time I actually need you to know something weird, you don't."

"The one time?"

"You know what I mean!"

"Flying a plane takes years of practice, and it's dangerous."

"Dangerous? You rode a motorcycle blindfolded down a hill!"

"That safety instructor dared me to! She was totally impressed."

"She also failed you on the test!"

"She still bought me a coffee later."

"You are hopeless."

"The point is, if you want to fly over the Verdes' ranch, you're going to need someone else to get us there."

"When we were cycling through the city, we passed at least three small airports. Which seemed weird, until I remembered what you said about all the rich people here."

"The kind with enough money to buy their own jets."

Neil nodded. "It reminded me of Nori, that crazy Japanese tycoon who tried to kill us."

"Anything that reminds you of that guy can't be good."

"It reminded me of the huge boat he had, with a runway and a private floatplane, helicopter, and submarine. He had them all close to where he lived."

Larry stopped packing and looked at Neil. "We did pass that one airfield, with the big houses built around it. . . ."

"Yes! The houses had garages for their planes the same way you might have one for a car."

"So you thought we should go break into one of the garages, hijack a small plane, and fly over the ranch. Why?"

"The trees. Something bugged me about them when we were leaving the ranch. Feleena said Guillermo had planted an olive tree each time a child or grandchild was born."

"So?"

"Well, when we were driving past the grove, there were close to a hundred trees."

"That's a lot of kids!"

"Too many. Let's be real. And not all of the trees were even close to a hundred years old."

"How can you tell?"

Neil tapped his nose. "I've visited plenty of olive groves, and old olive trees produce a distinctly different pollen and fruit than new trees."

"So the Verdes have been adding to the groves since Guillermo died."

Neil nodded. "There was even a two-year-old sapling by the house. Planted to honor Julio's wife."

"And if the trees Guillermo planted are still there?"

"They'll be in the heart of the grove. The true heart of the Verdes. Their family."

"You think he hid a clue in the trees?"

"Yes. I just don't know what it is. But if I can see the trees, how he planted them, maybe I can figure it all out."

Larry scratched his chin. "So you think those are the trees on the map?"

"Olive trees look a lot like broccoli, if they're drawn by someone who isn't an artist."

"Or maybe Guillermo planted some broccoli we're supposed to find. That's gonna be really tough after all these years."

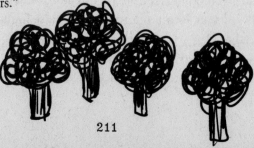

"So, now do you see why we need to get a plane, or a helicopter?"

"Can't we just sneak up and see the trees on the ground?"

"I'm willing to bet at least one armed guard is hiding *in* those trees."

Larry scratched his chin again. "Well, trying to fly a stolen plane over the farm is a sure way to get us noticed and shot down. And finding someone who hasn't read the papers to hire as a pilot is also an incredible long shot."

"That's why I was hoping you knew how to fly!"

Larry smiled. "I do have another skill that might come in handy. But it's going to require a little makeup and a trip to the mall."

Neil looked and felt ridiculous. It wasn't that he was wearing a dress. One of his favorite chefs, Mel Giblet, wore dresses and makeup all the time, and he and Neil had made a lot of money with their booth at the last Vancouver Pride rally.

It was more that the dress he and Larry had snatched from a laundry line was clearly way too small. Also, Neil had refused to take off his sneakers, and they didn't go with the outfit at all. They were starting to seriously smell.

He'd made some lipstick from a can of maraschino cherries they'd salvaged from the FrankenWagon. Larry had given him his retro-style sunglasses and then tucked his red hair into a tea towel that passed, almost, for a head scarf.

He looked like a demented mannequin.

No one seemed to notice too much out of the

ordinary, so Neil walked on looking for a Brickstones, the "Electronics Superstore."

"It's a chain. Every mall has one," Larry had said, and sure enough, Neil saw the glowing red sign up ahead.

He passed a security camera, mounted high up on a pillar, and did his best to hide his face while also not looking like he was hiding his face. He was pretty sure he failed. More reason to get moving.

Neil walked into the store and straight up to a display of exactly what he was looking for. A white drone, looking almost like a small helicopter with four rotors, sat on top of its box. Hanging on the wall were all the accessories and batteries Larry had written down on his shopping list.

Now if he could just pay and get out without having to talk to anyone. He reached for the box.

"May I be of assistance?" It was a young woman with a huge smile. Her name tag said I'M TAMMY! ASK ME ABOUT OUR AMMO!

The smile grew unsteady as Neil turned and gave a quick shake of his head.

"Are you okay, ma'am?" Tammy asked, putting a hand on Neil's shoulder. "Your lips look like they're bleeding."

"I'm fine," Neil croaked, hoping he sounded like a woman with a cold and not a kid whose voice was still breaking. "I just need . . ." Instead of straining to keep his voice weak, he just pointed repeatedly at the drones.

Tammy's smile reappeared. "Oh, the SpyFace 2000 is our top-of-the-line camera drone. And"—she leaned in close to Neil's ear—"it's also on sale for half-price. I'll even throw in the batteries."

Neil held his hand up to his face and nodded vigorously.

"But there's a catch," Tammy said. She reached out and grabbed the box. "This is the last one, and we have a tradition here at the store that everyone who buys the last of anything gets a spot on our Wall of Fame!"

She pointed to a wall of photos. In each one Tammy was standing next to some shocked-looking customer, giving a thumbs-up sign and smiling so much she looked like she was about to swallow a bird.

Neil froze and shook his head vigorously.

"Too bad," Tammy said. "It's a very popular model. But I'm sure someone else will buy it." She put the box back on the display rack.

Neil couldn't believe it. This was customer service? If the Soba twins had tried this at Chez Flambé, he would

have fired them on the spot. He wanted to get into an argument right then and there, but he knew he couldn't. Talking in his patented "outside voice" would blow his cover. Fast.

Instead he tapped Tammy on the shoulder and inclined his head, trying to silently convey that he was willing to pose for the photo, as long as she gave him back the drone.

"That's the spirit!" she said. She handed Neil the drone and then led him over to the wall. She pushed a button and a white curtain came down behind them and a camera rose from a hole in the floor.

"Just more of our miracle products," Tammy said with a smile.

Neil tried to make sure his face was as hidden as possible.

Just before the camera flash went off, Tammy reached over and took off his sunglasses.

"Can't have those covering up that . . . face." She looked almost on the verge of saying *pretty*, but even Neil could tell she couldn't pull off that lie. She handed him back the glasses, and he quickly put them on as Tammy walked over to the checkout.

"So, that'll be four hundred even," she said. "Cash or credit?"

Neil fumbled for the plastic bag he'd stuffed into his socks. He turned and counted out the money, knowing full well how suspicious he looked.

He handed Tammy the cash. Her smile stayed pasted on her face, but she put each and every bill under the counterfeit detection light.

Finally, satisfied his money was at least honest, she rang up the sale and put everything in a bag.

"There ya go, honey," she said. "Have a great day. And maybe get some better lipstick with all the money you saved!"

Neil nodded, took the bag, and quickly turned to leave the store.

Tammy called after him, "I'll also post that picture on our blog tonight! Tell your family and friends!"

Neil ducked his head and rushed as quickly as he could to the parking lot.

CHAPTER THIRTY

BIRD'S-EYE VIEW

Larry lay as flat as he could against the rocks and played with the levers on the control pad. The drone took off, humming and whirring as the propellers spun faster and faster. Neil and Larry were crouched on the rim of the crater, overlooking the ranch. They'd biked up in the middle of the night, then waited until first light to try their plan.

"I love these things," Larry said. "Have you seen any of the videos I shot last year of our soccer practices?"

"It will not surprise you in least when I say I'd rather have a drone smash into my face."

"That's exactly what happened to Doug, our goalie! He thought it was a ball, dove to make the save, and *whammo*, right in the kisser. That video actually went viral. Helped me pay for his dental work."

"Look, I'm glad you have hobbies, especially right now, but can we focus?"

Larry responded by buzzing Neil with the drone. "The look on your face there was classic! I hope the camera got it all!"

"We don't need videos of me. We need to see those trees."

"Practice makes perfect."

A bird gave a loud squawk.

Neil crouched down. "Why do we have to be so close?"

"We're not *that* close. You got the best drone on the market. This baby has a range of, like, half a mile."

"Half a mile?"

"What, you had some idea that we could sit safely in New Mexico and fly the robot camera over the ranch while sipping freshly squeezed organic orange juice?"

"That's a pretty specific jab."

"Was I right about the orange juice?"

"Yes."

"Anyway, they aren't looking for us way up here. And if we do this right, they'll never even hear or see the drone."

"I don't like the word 'if' in this scenario."

"Fine, *when* we do this right. We can sneak in and sneak out with some high-def pics of the ranch and the olive grove. If we're lucky, we might even figure out where the guys with the guns are hiding."

Neil took a deep breath. He felt like *he* was about to go flying over the ranch. The whirring of the rotors was uncomfortably loud as the drone lifted up in the air.

"Will it get quieter?" he asked.

"Once it's up in the sky, they won't hear it."

Larry sent the drone straight up for about a minute and then pushed the control levers forward, sending it speeding toward the distant ranch.

"How do you know what the drone is seeing?"

Larry pointed to a small screen on the control panel. "The images in the actual camera will be way better, but this gives us a rough idea of what we're looking at."

Neil leaned in close to Larry and stared at the screen. Right now it was just showing the green and golden fields of the ranch. Then Neil saw a red block.

"That's the roofing tiles from the ranch house," Larry said.

He played with the levers, and the drone flew a little lower. Neil saw fuzzy figures moving around in the front of the house. It was hard to tell from the images, but they seemed to be bumping up against one another. Finally two of them got into a blue blob—Neil assumed it was a car or truck—and drove away.

"I can't wait to see what's actually going on there," Neil said.

"Once we get the camera back, we'll look. Okay, how far up the driveway was this olive grove?"

"We passed it just inside the front gates."

"So another hundred yards or so."

Larry gently nudged the levers, and the image followed the line of the driveway until another mass of green showed up on the screen.

"It does look like broccoli!" Larry said.

"Can you get closer? We've probably got just one shot at this, and I want to make sure we can see it clearly."

Larry lowered the drone closer to the green mass. As it got lower, Neil could make out the edge of the driveway more clearly.

The blue blob had stopped. One of the figures had gotten out and was standing still. The drone lowered more and Neil saw that whoever it was appeared to be looking up and pointing at the sky.

"Uh-oh," Neil said.

There was a small flash and the image on the screen suddenly spun. Now sky. Now ground. Then it went black.

"Is it dead?" Neil said, panicked.

Larry continued to play with the controls. "I don't think so. These controls vibrate if the drone is still responding."

"Wait! Send it west!" Neil said.

"Why?"

"If they saw the drone, they'll be watching where it goes. Send it way west and then bring it back here after it's passed out of sight."

"I hope it has enough juice!"

Neil grabbed the binoculars. "Where should I look?"

Larry pointed straight ahead. "It should be heading west, straight out from the ranch house. You'll see it soon."

Neil dug his elbows into the ground and focused his attention on the sky above the ranch. He scanned the clouds, and even got tricked by some birds, but he finally caught sight of the drone. It was wobbling in the air, sinking and rising erratically.

Neil zoomed in. "One of the rotors has been ripped apart."

"I'm going to go out on a limb and suggest that Aprende was the guy we saw on the ground."

"And he knows we're close." Neil punched the ground. "Back to plan A. Let's get that drone and get out of here."

"Roger that," Larry said. He played with the controls and the drone began heading straight toward them.

"Faster!" Neil said.

The drone came at them. Larry caught sight of it. "Looks like a sick bumblebee."

"Just get it here!" Neil could see a dust plume on the grounds of the ranch. The blue blob was following the drone and was heading straight for them. Then Neil saw the flashing lights and they heard the wailing siren. "Now!"

Larry sent the drone rising up above them, then cut the power. The drone fell and crashed on the rocks, sending plastic and metal shards skittering across the ground.

"Leave the drone, grab the camera," Larry said.

Neil grabbed the camera and ran to his bike. "Now what?"

"We get the heck out of here and see what the olive trees are hiding."

They sped away, sending rocks flying.

CHAPTER THIRTY-ONE

SCREEN TIME

In what way are we 'beyond the long arm of the law' here?" Neil asked. He and Larry were sitting in a cave on the edge of a cliff, their bikes stowed in a nearby creek bed.

"We walked up that creek for at least an hour, covering our tracks," Larry said. "Just like Butch Cassidy and the Sundance Kid."

"My dad made me watch that movie once. Don't they both get shot?"

"Relax, cuz. Even if the cops followed the drone to the rim, it's way too steep to drive up. They would still have to go back out the way they came, out the front gate of the ranch, then turn, then come back to where we were an hour ago. And we can see anyone coming a mile away from here, and they can't see us."

Neil nervously scanned the horizon with the binoculars, and Larry fiddled with the camera.

"Is it broken?" Neil asked.

"Yes and no. The internal stuff is fine. It's just that the impact bent the case, so I can't get the buttons to respond. I'll have to jam it open and get the memory card out."

"Then what?"

"You got that adapter thingamabob I asked for?"

"Yes. Although calling it that on the shopping list wasn't a huge help." Neil reached into the shopping bag, grabbed a tiny white box, and tossed it at Larry. "Luckily, it was right next to the drone stuff, so I figured this was what you meant."

"Perfect! I just plug this into my phone, making sure my signal is still turned off, and then presto, we can see the pics . . . well, once I extract the memory card and plug it into the adapter."

Neil went back to scanning the horizon as Larry attacked the camera with a rock, then a series of rocks. He even went back in and out of the cave a few times, amassing a whole pile of larger and larger ones.

"Try throwing it off the cliff," Neil joked.

"Trust me, I'm thinking of it." Larry continued cracking the case with a rock. "Finally!"

Neil looked over. The lens casing had cracked, a little. Larry concentrated on the crack, making it bigger and bigger. It split in half, and a tiny computer chip flew out and bounced across the ground. "Don't lose that!" Larry yelled.

Neil tried to snatch it, but it glanced off his fingers and out of the mouth of the cave.

"Nice reflexes, chef boy," Larry said.

"You sent it flying, not me!" Neil said. "Now what?"

"I'll go get it," Larry said. "Is the coast clear?"

Neil looked through the binoculars and saw the last thing he wanted to see, a rising plume of dust, headed straight for the mountain.

"No."

Larry fell to the ground. "Maybe they'll keep going past."

The car didn't go by but began to slow down. Then it stopped, right below them. Aprende got out of the passenger side and stared up at the side of the mountain, scanning it with his eyes. Neil crept back but kept the binoculars fixed on the sheriff. Aprende pulled something small out of his pocket and looked from it back up the mountain, then he did it again and again, each time focusing in more and more on Neil and Larry's hiding place.

Whippet got out of the driver's side, holding a rifle. Aprende looked at the device, then pointed, right at the opening to the cave.

"He's got another tracking device!" Neil hissed.

"How?"

"I don't know," Neil said. "Your duffel bag?"

"I checked that inside and out. Impossible."

Whippet kept the rifle fixed on the cave. If Neil or Larry tried to escape, they'd be shot. Aprende began walking up the side of the mountain. He carried a megaphone, and as he got closer, he turned it on. "Nice hiding, boys. I've got to hand it to you, you have pulled the wool over these eyes again and again, but that stops now."

"Baaaaaaa," Larry called.

"Very funny. Very funny indeed. Now, I'm gonna end this. You're trapped. Whippet's got a bead on you in case you move, and I've got two bullets with your names on them once I reach that cave. So, start saying your prayers."

"You are a good tracker," Larry yelled. "I'll die impressed."

"Ain't no special trick. I rely on my own noggin to a point, and then modern technology helps me and my horse cross the bridge the rest of the way."

"What the heck does that even mean?"

"Flying a drone without a permit is illegal. So each drone is equipped with a homing device. That way we can find it and blast it out of the sky, or track it back to the idiot who's decided to fly one."

"How did you even know we had a drone?"

"Next time your redheaded partner gets his picture taken and posted online, tell him to do a better job with the makeup. I found that pic within minutes using facial recognition software."

Neil hadn't spoken the whole time. Instead he tried to inch forward as carefully as he could, looking for the computer chip and gauging how

long it would take before Aprende reached them.

He saw the chip, just out of reach, sitting on a flat rock. If Neil tried to get it, he'd certainly expose himself to Whippet's aim. Aprende was only a few minutes away.

Neil slunk back in and sidled next to Larry. "I think I've got one more plan for the scuba gear."

"What?"

Neil motioned toward the pile of rocks Larry had collected to use on the camera.

A smile spread across Larry's face. "Slingshots. Sort of like the ones we used in Paris!"

Neil nodded. "Aprende has a six-shooter, and he's going to have to come very close to get at us. We'll be waiting. It's our only chance."

Larry grabbed the masks from the duffel bag, tore off the mouthpieces, and handed one to Neil. Then they settled against the wall of the cave and pulled back the straps, loading the masks with the biggest rocks they could find.

Neil could hear Aprende scratching his way closer. The rubber straps vibrated between his fingertips. He turned to Larry. "If we get out of this, and we travel together again, we are definitely packing scuba gear."

Larry smiled. "Only if we visit the desert again."

They heard the sound of a gun being cocked, and Aprende's black hat rose above the lip of the cave.

Neil was about to let go with his rock, but Larry whispered, "Wait. Wait until you see his eyes."

The hat continued to rise and then Neil saw that Aprende was using a stick to lift it. He wiggled the stick, making the hat wobble around. Then he laughed.

"Well, that makes me feel a lot better. Now I knows you ain't armed." The hat lowered and then rose again, this time with Aprende's head inside.

Larry unleashed his rock. It hit Aprende square in the forehead. His eyes rolled back in his head. Neil and Larry launched more rocks. They hit Aprende so hard his hat flew off his head. He fell backward. Neil rushed to the lip of the cave. Aprende was tumbling down the side of the mountain, his guns flying away from his hands. Whippet had lowered his rifle and was rushing toward where Aprende was falling.

"Whippet's not looking!" Neil yelled.

Larry jumped out of the cave and began running up the hill toward the bikes. "C'mon, Neil!"

Neil was looking for the memory card. Aprende must have knocked it away when he fell. Neil quickly got down on his hands and knees and felt around between the loose rocks and grass.

He saw something glint in the sunlight a few feet away and he jumped for it. He grabbed the card. A gunshot ricocheted off the ground next to him. It missed, but a shard of stone struck Neil in the arm.

He grabbed his arm and yelled in pain as another shot hit the rocks near his head. Whippet was charging up the hill, firing repeatedly. Aprende continued to roll down toward him.

Neil scrambled to follow Larry, as the shots got closer and closer. He was too exposed. He'd never make it to the creek bed before Whippet narrowed his aim.

"Larry, I've got the chip!"

Larry burst from the bushes, rolling a huge rock. He heaved, and it cascaded down toward Whippet.

Whippet fired again, but the shot went far over their heads. Then he turned and ran back down the hill. Aprende was now lying motionless in a heap near the bottom. The boulder picked up more and more rocks and soon there was a mini avalanche, sending up a cloud of dust.

Whippet and Aprende disappeared in the haze.

"That's our cue to get out of here," Larry said. "Let's get that arm bandaged and move while they can't see us."

Neil nodded but gritted his teeth in pain.

Larry helped Neil stand. They skittered up the hill and then down into the creek bed. Larry had the bikes ready to go. He took off his me-shirt and tied it around Neil's arm.

Neil looked at the makeshift tourniquet and frowned.

"You told me your me-shirt said 'Cowboy? No. CowMAN!'"

Larry didn't answer. He just grinned and pedaled off on his bike.

Neil looked at the shirt again. The words CHEFS ARE CRACKED were clearly emblazoned in white script over a picture of Neil as an egg.

CHAPTER THIRTY-TWO

FOREST FOR THE TREES

And now time for the show!" Larry said, powering up his cell phone. "I wish we had some popcorn. Any wild plants that are similar?"

"I'm not leaving the shelter to look for anything," Neil said. They'd pedaled for hours, expecting sirens, helicopters, or even missiles to come out of nowhere at any second. After numerous spills, unexpected dips, and scraping their arms on rocks, they'd finally ridden into some hills.

Thunderclouds turned the sky dark.

"We'd better find cover," Larry said.

Neil scanned the hillside. He spied a cave about a hundred feet up.

"There," Neil said, pointing.

They'd slipped inside just as the storm hit.

To their surprise and joy, the small opening had actually led to a larger room inside.

"Okay, then it's beans again." Larry's phone lit up just as he grabbed a can of beans. "Well, lefty, you can open the can while I see what's on this memory chip."

Neil flipped the tab on top of the beans but then caught a whiff of something else. Something like wheat, or maybe, actually, popcorn kernels. He shook his head, but when he sniffed the air again, the smell was still there.

Where was it coming from?

While Larry fiddled with his phone, Neil began crawling around the floor, sniffing like a bloodhound. The smell was coming from the back of the cave. Neil inched closer. It was solid rock, but the smell, though incredibly faint, was coming from there.

"Larry, flash the light over here."

Larry was still trying to figure out how to fit the chip into the adapter, but he pointed the phone's screen at the wall. Now that it was lit up, Neil could see that it wasn't solid rock, but a solid wall of adobe. It looked like rock at first glance, but once he got up close and ran his hand over it, he could tell it was just clever camouflage.

Neil tapped the wall. There was a hollow sound.

"That's weird," Larry said.

"Yeah." Neil's stomach growled loudly.

"Your super stomach senses food is near!" Larry said. He gave up on the phone for a second and joined Neil at the wall.

"So what is this place?"

"I don't know. But I can smell something better than beans."

Neil began scratching at the wall but only succeeded in scraping his fingers.

"Try this," Larry said, handing Neil his pocketknife.

"Thanks." Neil scratched and stabbed at the spot where the wall met the floor. After a few minutes he succeeded in making a small crack. The smell of grains and corn intensified.

"I've got the camera chip working," Larry said.

"In a minute." Neil continued to hack away at the crack, making it larger bit by bit. Finally, it was big enough to get down and peer through. "Larry, give me the phone."

Larry took out the chip and handed him the phone. "Don't break it."

Neil stuck it into the hole and took a picture. He pulled out the phone, and he and Larry looked. On the other side of the wall were about a dozen jars of pottery, with painted patterns in red, black, and white. Two of them were broken, spilling grains and corn kernels all over the floor.

"Those are the ones I smelled," Neil said. "But I bet the other jars are sealed. That stuff might still be edible."

"Like the honey Lord Lane gave us?"

"Don't remind me," Neil said. The only good thing that had come out of their last case, as far as he was concerned, was the passing grade he'd gotten on a Shakespeare quiz, without having to study.

"What are we waiting for?!" Larry and Neil began chipping away with the knife, then stones. Soon they were able to pull chunks of the adobe away. The pottery was sitting on wood-and-stone shelves. The wood had dried and broken on the bottom shelf and the two jars had fallen. Neil looked closer. Some of the jars weren't pottery at all but were made of finely woven tree branches and leaves.

"It looks like a storage room. Sort of a pantry. But it's really old. Look at all the dust on the jars."

"It was probably like an emergency food supply for a village or something."

Neil's stomach grumbled again. "Well, we are in that situation now. We can open one and see if it's still edible."

"Let's leave most of them alone," Larry said. "I'll bet a museum would love to know about this place."

"We'll draw them a map with some broccoli and a recipe for skillet cake."

"That is a horrible idea," Larry said, smiling. "So, chef boy, which one contains the popcorn?"

Neil looked at the patterns on the jars. The broken one with the corn kernels had a kind of checkmark pattern made of black fibers. There was a perfect match on the shelves. "That one."

The storm passed. Neil and Larry found some wood, and a few minutes later Neil had a small fire going. Larry had eaten the last of the beans, and then Neil poked holes in the can. He filled it a quarter full with corn kernels and was now doing his best to heat the can evenly. Of course, Neil's best was always excellent, so in a short time the smell of roasting, popping corn filled their shelter.

"All right! Showtime," Larry said, munching on the corn.

He sat the phone on a rock, inserted the chip, and then pressed play.

The video showed the fields of the ranch, with cows and sheep grazing happily.

"The quality is actually really good," Neil said. "But maybe skip to the trees."

Larry reached for the phone and stopped. The screen clearly showed an image of Feleena and Julio being dragged from the ranch house by Aprende and Whippet.

Then Aprende pointed something at them, and there was a flash.

Julio fell to the ground.

Feleena got on her knees next to him. Aprende raised his hand again. Then the drone passed over the scene and toward the olive trees.

Larry pressed pause and sat back, stunned. "Did I just see what I think I saw?"

Neil fought back angry tears, his lips trembling. He punched the ground. "What was even the point of that? Aprende and Whippet are winning. We're nowhere near finding this stupid mine. They'd be getting the ranch anyway. Why do that? What possible reason . . ." A horrible feeling washed over him.

"Oh no," he said. "Aprende shot them because they were protecting us."

"How?"

"Remember when Feleena called, she told us her dad was refusing to say where we'd headed? It didn't matter then, because Aprende had somehow already stuck a homing device in my bag."

"But now that we were back off his radar screen, he

needed some actual help from Julio." Larry stared back at the screen, the image of Aprende's car frozen there. "I guess this means Feleena and Julio were on our side all along."

"And to think I gave any credit to that stupid story Whippet told us in the desert." Neil hung his head and sighed. "Now I really want to find that mine. I want to expose these jerks for what they are."

"Or were, if that rockslide was as bad as it looked," Larry said.

"Let's see what the trees look like," Neil said.

Larry pressed play. The drone continued to fly down the driveway, then reached the olive grove. "This is where I lowered the drone," he said. The screen was soon filled with the green of the trees.

Neil leaned in and stared at the screen. "Pause it here," he said. "Can you zoom?"

Larry tapped the image and the trees became even clearer. Neil looked closely at the grove. It was just a jumble of olive leaves and branches. He frowned. "Maybe zoom out?"

Larry tapped again and the grove grew smaller and smaller. "Wait!" Neil called. "Freeze it!"

He grabbed the phone and stared at the screen. From farther away it was clear. There was a definite pattern of older, more deep green olive trees, surrounded by a circle of lighter green, younger trees.

"The pure heart of the Verdes," Neil said, holding the phone up so Larry could see.

The pattern was an arrow.

The arrow was pointing south.

CHAPTER THIRTY-THREE

GONE SOUTH

Neil and Larry didn't wait for morning but got back on their bikes and began pedaling as fast as they could. The arrow was pointing due south of the ranch.

"The trees didn't happen to say how far south we needed to go, did they?" Larry asked.

"Nope. But I think Guillermo is pretty sure that whoever heads that way will find the mountain and know it by sight."

"Unless they were looking for a valley," Larry said. "In which case they'd never have found the right place."

"That was the 'great skill' part of Guillermo's message."

"And you, my cheffy friend, have yet again shown the great skill of a great chef. This Guillermo must have been pretty talented."

"He would have been fun to meet."

They rode on in silence for a long time.

"Something is really bumming me out," Larry said after

they'd stopped for a drink and a snack, more pre-popped popcorn à la Flambé.

"The homing beacon and the poisoned barbecue sauce?"

"Great minds clearly think about shady things alike. Both were inside jobs."

Neil nodded. "Had to be. After I heard Whippet's story, I thought it might have been Feleena and Julio. Maybe they had set us up, making sure that they'd get the treasure and we'd get thrown in jail. I'd like to apologize to them."

"Don't feel bad. They had the opportunity. And Whippet gave us a possible motive. But if it wasn't either of them . . ."

"It had to be one of the other chefs. One of them was planted by Aprende."

"To frame us."

Neil thought for a moment. "I'm not so sure about that. Maybe they were just supposed to ruin the festival, maybe poison someone and frame the Verdes. It would have been one more thing that went wrong for them, maybe the last straw."

"Then Aprende worried we were actually on the right path. So he had them frame us instead."

"Who would think one person could be so twisted?"

"Two people. Remember, he and Whippet have been working this whole thing together. They both have a little Gravestone in them, if you ask me."

Neil nodded. "Hey, wait a minute. Maybe they actually do both have a little Gravestone in them. Maybe they're related."

"Brothers?"

"Or cousins? I don't know. But why else would a police officer, even a crazed lunatic police officer, be helping out so much? I think they both want revenge."

Larry munched the last of the popcorn.

Neil thought about the brush with death they'd had on the cliff the day before. "Do you think we killed him and Whippet?"

Larry didn't answer right away. He chewed his popcorn slowly and then swallowed.

"I hope not, but he didn't look too good lying there."

"I hope not too." Neil sat there, feeling horrible. "Larry, this is it. I know that I've sworn off the detective stuff before, but this time I'm done. I'm sick of it. And without all my friends here to help, it's worse."

"You got me here."

"You know what I mean." Neil felt a lump in his throat. "I would way rather be driving around in a food truck with you than almost anything right now."

Larry gave a little laugh. "Neil Flambé in a food truck. Who'd have thought? I mean, that was just an experiment for the Broiling Man Festival, but you actually, and I mean actually, liked that?"

Neil paused. It was almost the exact opposite of how he had seen his future. He had always seen himself as top chef, in charge of a line of five-star restaurants, famous, rich. He'd have the best of everything.

Was driving around in a hunk of junk, with his crazy cousin, really as good?

Neil shook his head, hardly believing what he was about to say. "Yeah, I did. Actually. Actually, a lot."

Larry beamed. "Wow. Well, once we find this mine, I say we find the FrankenWagon and fix her up. Then we just drive around BC and the US, wowing people with our amazing Flambé Fanstasticalness!"

"Okay. But no hammocks."

"Party pooper."

"And maybe let's actually find the mine first."

"Good idea. I say we pedal until the sun comes up. We've been heading due south, if my star reading is right, and haven't bumped into anything. We'll see what we can see at dawn, and then find a safe place to sleep."

"Deal."

They pedaled, and still didn't hit any peaks, until the sun came up. The first glimmer of yellow light broke on the horizon. They stopped and rested on a rock.

"Isn't this what lizards do?" Larry asked.

"Right before they die from exhaustion." Neil took off his helmet and watched the sunlight lick the sky.

Neil could see large masses on the horizon, but they were too indistinct to make out much detail.

He could barely keep his eyes open, but he forced himself to stay awake as the sunlight began to creep up the side of the distant peaks and hills.

Larry began making loud drumming and then humming noises.

"What are you doing?"

"I'm humming the *2001* theme."

"The what?"

"The movie *2001*. There're all these monkeys in a desert and then the sun comes up and there's this big black box and they all start dancing around it. And this awesome music is playing, and it's like human beings are being born for the first time, and then there's this floating spaceship. . . ."

Neil looked at Larry like he was crazy.

"It's, like, the best movie ever made."

"I'll take your word for it," Neil said.

"You have so much to learn," Larry said, shaking his head sadly. "As soon as we get back to civilization, we are going to watch this movie and then . . ."

Neil wasn't paying attention anymore. He was slowly standing, watching as the sun first suggested, then confirmed that they were not far from the base of a mountain.

The pink sunlight grew more and more intense, outlining the peak more and more clearly with each passing second.

"Oh my," Neil said, his face beginning to break out in a smile.

Larry stood up next to him, humming the theme from *2001* louder and louder until the sun made the top of the mountain shine out like the light on a lighthouse. It was the valley from the map, turned completely upside down.

"Daaa, DAAA, DDDDDDAAAAAAAAAAAA-AHHHHHHHHHHH!" Larry sang.

"Guillermo's mountain!" Neil said, almost too shocked to speak.

He took a step forward. The mountain seemed so close he could reach out and touch it.

"Whoa, Neil. That sun is making us just as visible as the mountain. We should wait until the sun goes down."

Neil didn't stop walking. "No. We're too close to stop."

"If they see us, they'll attack us and then go find the mine."

Neil stopped.

Larry put a hand on his shoulder. "Remember, we're the only people in the world who know what we're looking at. Aprende and Whippet still think we're looking for a valley."

Neil turned around.

"C'mon, Slappy. Let's get some sleep."

"Okay. But as soon as the sun starts going down, we're going hiking."

Larry smiled. "Now let's find a safe place to get some rest."

They began walking their bikes toward a stand of rocks a few yards away. Neil couldn't take his eyes off the mountain. Something inside was calling him. He wondered if he'd even be able to sleep.

CHAPTER THIRTY-FOUR

OUCH

"Ouch!" Neil said. He'd brushed his hand against a tiny cactus. "Maybe groping around in the dark was not exactly the best plan."

"You could do what I'm doing and sit on a rock."

"No thanks. I'm going to keep moving. The last thing I need is a scorpion sneaking up on me and stinging my butt."

"That is not going to happen. No scorpion is that desperate."

"Ha."

"The moon will be out soon, and then we'll get a better look," Larry said. "Remember, we want this place kept a secret. Two guys with flashlights might arouse suspicion, if there is anybody around."

"Fine." Neil grumbled. "Ouch!" he said, brushing against yet another cactus.

"Be more careful where you're

walking. We're just getting into position and then we'll look for the mine."

"It's a big mountain."

"This from the guy who thought the Grand Canyon was a ditch."

"That was before I saw it!"

"Look, we'll do this methodically. Once the moon comes out, we start zigzagging up this side of the mountain. If we don't find anything, we do it again tomorrow to the west, and so on until we come across it."

"And if we don't?"

"Then we'll risk it in daylight."

The moon began rising, and Neil could see the outlines of the rocks and cacti more clearly.

Larry stood up. "So, we are looking for a couple of egg-shaped boulders?"

"That seems to be right. I didn't see any likely candidates through the binoculars when we were camped."

"So maybe let's head a little to the western side and start from there."

They used the moonlight to guide their steps. There were many small rocks, ledges, even some small openings for caves, but nothing that fit the description from Feleena's story.

The moon began to set.

"This is hopeless," Neil said. "We've been looking for hours."

"What do you expect? The mine has stayed hidden for a hundred years. It's not going to be something you can stumble on by accident."

Despite his paranoia, Neil sat down to rest. This was

going to take a lot longer than he'd thought. It wasn't that he was expecting to magically discover the mine right away, but he had been hoping there would be some other sign on the mountain to suggest where they should look.

Something a chef with a super-nose might be able to discover.

He sat up. Wait. There had been a scent when they'd "discovered" the mine in the Grand Canyon. There had been the smell of bat poop. He could keep searching with his nose even after the moon disappeared.

Neil stood up and stuck his nose in the air. Nothing yet!

"Larry! We don't need to look."

"What do you mean?" Larry called, scrambling over from the rocks he'd been searching.

"I don't need to look. I just need to smell."

"You haven't showered in a week. Trust me, you smell."

"That joke was too easy, even for you. What I mean is that there should be a whole pile of bat poop in the mine. If I could smell it in the canyon, I should be able to smell it here."

"Go smell some poop!"

Neil found he could cover way more ground searching this way. He just needed to figure out where the breeze was and then stay in one place, sniffing the air.

Even still, they walked and walked with no sign of anything but the smells of cactus flowers and dust.

Larry stared at the horizon and saw a sliver of yellow begin to burn on the horizon. "Neil, the sun's going to be up soon." Then a loud boom echoed in the distance.

"And there's another storm brewing. We've got to find some cover."

"Just two more minutes."

Another boom of thunder, closer.

"One minute."

Neil walked more quickly, trying to smell as much air as he could.

Then there was a flash of lightning, with the thunder not far behind.

"Time's up. We've got to find shelter, and we've got to find it soon."

A few drops of rain began to pelt the dirt at their feet. The sun was shining in the narrow gap between the horizon and the bottom of the storm cloud.

The wind picked up and then changed direction. And Neil caught the scent. Bat poop, carried on the wind.

"There it is!" he said. He began rushing headlong into the wind, the smell growing stronger with each step. Neil just needed the wind to keep howling.

A lightning bolt struck the land about a mile away, and he could feel the thunder pound against his chest.

"Hurry!" Larry said, following close behind. The sun rose into the clouds, and they were thrown back into near darkness.

Neil ran and ran, as the rain began to fall. The wind whipped it into his face, but he focused on the bats, despite the ozone and the new smell of released creosote.

There was another flash and then thunder at the same time.

"This is not a good situation," Larry yelled over the

wind and rain. "Just find us someplace to hide!"

"I just did!" Neil yelled back. The lightning had illuminated two large boulders, now nearly covered in bushes, and Neil could smell the heavy scent of a cave full of bat poop.

"I don't care if that's the mine or a sewer, let's go!"

Neil scrambled over as another bolt of lightning struck the peak above them. The thunder was deafening. A few rocks that had been loosened by the blast rolled past them and down toward the desert floor.

"It's here for sure," Neil yelled, searching the rocks for any way inside.

"Try the top!" Larry said. He ran over and helped boost Neil on top of the rock. Neil could see a large hole, big enough for a teenage chef for sure.

He turned back, smiling. "Good idea. Follow me."

Neil reached back and helped Larry climb up the slick boulder.

Completely soaked, they sat back down and slid into the hole and right into a giant pile of rain-soaked poop.

Neil hadn't been happier in days.

The rain dripped repeatedly into the hole. A puddle was forming at the base of the boulders. Larry pointed. "Erosion."

"Just like it was in the canyon."

"That whole excursion was like a dry run for the real thing."

Neil looked at his soaked shirt. "I guess that makes this a wet run."

"Ha!"

Neil peered into the cave. It was dark and damp and filled, as far as he could smell, with even more poop. He could also sense a slight breeze as the air traveled past them and out over the boulder.

"That means that unlike the cave in the canyon, this one has a hole at either end. So you get a draft."

"Let's go spelunk!" Larry beamed. He turned on the flashlight and pointed it into the darkness. The cave stretched back and then made a turn. It was only wide enough for them to go single file.

"I'll go in front with the light," Larry said. He began walking through the muck. Neil followed, his sneakers sinking into the ground. He had to pull them up carefully after each step to keep them from getting sucked off his feet.

"Larry, angle the light down for a second. I want to see how much of this we have to walk through. Yuck."

Larry pointed the light at the ground. "Neil. Look!" he said.

Neil stared at the pool of light. Stretching out ahead of them and around the corner was a clear set of footprints.

CHAPTER THIRTY-FIVE

FOLLOWING IN THE FOOTSTEPS

A shiver ran down Neil's spine. "We're not alone," he whispered.

"You've had that feeling this whole adventure."

"And I've been right."

"This time I'm not so sure." Larry knelt down to get a closer look at the prints. Then he stood back up, smiling.

"These are definitely footprints, but they've been partially filled up with bat poop. I'm going to guess about a hundred years' worth."

Neil leaned around Larry and stared at the single line of prints, heading only into the cave. There were no footprints coming the other way.

"Guillermo," they said together.

Neil thought he felt the breeze grew slightly colder

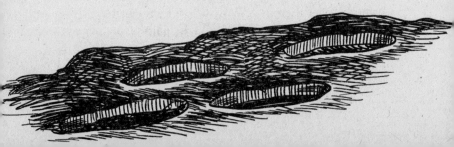

and stronger as they said his name. He had felt like he'd been following in the chef's footsteps for days, and now he definitely was.

"Before we go any farther," Neil said, "do we have a rope, or a way to get back up if we fall down another hole?"

Larry shook his head. "Nope. The last one we had was the one we left behind in the canyon with Gravestone's body. This is a one-way trip."

Neil nodded.

They did their best to step into the indentations Guillermo's boots had left behind. They turned the corner. Neil held his breath, half expecting to see Guillermo's ghostly figure standing in their path. Or Gravestone's. Or maybe even Aprende's.

"All clear?" Neil asked.

"I was tempted to say 'boo' but thought it best to keep you from dying of a heart attack."

"Thanks."

"But I can tell you that the footsteps disappear a short way ahead. And there's a big hole."

"I'm still a little worried about what we'll find down there."

"Maybe there is no gold?"

"Maybe. Or maybe there is no skillet."

"There's only one way to find out."

Larry took a step forward and stopped on the edge of the hole. "Guillermo's footprints slip here. I think that smudge over there is actually where he might have tried to grab ahold of something before he fell."

"Feleena said he had a light, at least when he was in the actual mine."

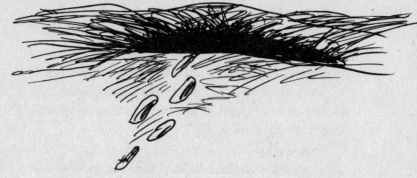

"I'll bet he didn't want to light it up here in case Gravestone was following him. Then he just fell in."

"Can you see the bottom?"

Larry leaned over the edge and stared down, even pointing the flashlight. "Nope. But it's not a straight drop, either. There's a bend about twenty feet down. Sort of like the way a slide bends at a water park."

"Except no water."

"Just manure."

"Great. Well, away we go."

"I'll go first," Larry said. "I'll call up and let you know if it's safe."

Neil reached out and hugged his cousin, holding him tightly.

"Good luck," he said.

Larry handed Neil his phone. "In case I don't call, you might need this." Larry sat on the edge of the hole and then slipped down. Neil could hear him yelling, "Whhhheeeeeeeeeee!" and then the cheering stopped.

"Larry, you good? LARRY?"

Neil listened intently but heard nothing.

"LAARRRYYY!" Neil turned on the phone's light and shone it down the hole.

"BOO!!" Larry yelled. His voice carried up the hole almost as if he were standing next to Neil.

"That's not funny!"

"Sorry, couldn't resist. Look, slide down like I did, but the bottom is a little bumpier than the rest, so get ready for that."

Neil sat on the edge of the hole and then pushed off. He gripped the phone tightly as the walls of the hole passed over his head. It was like being in a water slide, except that he could feel his rear end alternating between bumpy rock and soft gushiness.

This was not a hole you could climb back up.

Then the tunnel made an abrupt drop and Neil was flung against the wall. "Ouch!" he said, his shoulder crunching against the rock. He almost lost the grip on the phone but held it tightly in his palm. Then he fell straight down, landing on a bed of muck.

"That hurt!" he said.

"Told you." Larry was holding the flashlight in his hand. "It even broke the bulb in this thing."

Neil got up and opened his palm. The light, still on, began spreading through his fingers, revealing more and more of the walls. Just as in Feleena's story, it was stunning. The walls glittered like a thousand stars. Thick veins of gold ran through the rock.

Neil was speechless.

Larry wasn't. "Holy moly! I think we can safely say we have found the Lost Cook's Mine!"

Neil reached out and touched the closest wall.

"This isn't pyrite?"

Larry reached down and picked up a nugget and tossed it at Neil. It weighed more than Neil expected, and felt like . . . gold. There was a heaviness to it, a smoothness. It hadn't tarnished despite years of sitting exposed on the cave floor.

"That is definitely gold," Larry said.

Neil's face broke into an enormous smile. He began dancing around, pumping his legs up and down.

"Please, either stop that or turn off the light," Larry said, staring at him with a disgusted look on his face. "And don't *ever* show Isabella that dance move if you want to keep her around."

Neil kept dancing. "Even your sarcasm can't make me feel bad! We found it. WE FOUND IT!"

Larry's face softened, and he ran over and began dancing with Neil.

"I hope the camera isn't rolling on that thing!" Larry said, nodding at the phone.

Neil held it up and gulped. "No. But the cell data is!" He showed it to Larry.

"What? How?"

"I must have hit something when I was heading down the tunnel." Neil began frantically clicking buttons on the side of the phone, and then began tapping it against his hand, trying to re-create whatever he might have done in the tunnel.

"Don't break it! We need the light." Larry grabbed the phone and turned off the data with a series of finger taps.

"Whew," Neil said. "Sorry about that."

"Okay, we need to find that skillet and then get the heck out of here."

"There's no signal down here," Neil said.

"But there might have been up top. We shouldn't risk it. So let's get searching."

The cave was bigger than they'd expected. In addition to gold, there were amazing stalactites and stalagmites everywhere, like giant pillars of multicolored ice cream.

"This place is amazing!" Neil said. "It must be worth millions!"

"It's not worth anything unless we find that skillet."

They kicked aside rocks and mounds of "mud" and found more gold at every step, but no skillet. They searched the main room and the many smaller rooms that shot off the main cave.

"Was that part of the story not true?" Neil wondered.

Larry scratched his chin. "Both Feleena and Whippet mention the skillet. So it's not just made up."

"So that skillet has to be here, somewhere."

Neil stared all around, even looking at the ceiling. "Remember, in the story, Guillermo didn't know where he'd lost it. He just assumed he'd left it when he was grabbing all the gold. Maybe he was wrong."

"Meaning?"

"Meaning that Guillermo might not have left it on the ground, forgotten. Maybe it just fell off as he left the mine. He still lost it because he was greedy, but not in the way he thought or remembered."

A screen came up on Larry's phone. "Battery power at less than twenty percent," he read. "We'd better get out of here. I can recharge the phone with that solar thing you bought, but I don't see much sunlight down here. We can come back in later."

"So which way do we go?"

"Which way is that breeze coming from? Guillermo told his family that the bats showed him the way out. So let's use the same logic."

"Think like a bat? That should be easy for you," Neil joked.

"Ha. Also, I'd suggest we look for any sign of footprints. The ground down here is rockier than up top, but if he was following bats, he was probably following what they left behind, too."

They searched around and found a crack in the wall of a side room. The breeze was being channeled through, and there were faint footprints in the muck just inside the crack.

"That's a tight squeeze," Neil said. He sucked in his breath and crept inside, walking sideways.

"Turn off the light when you don't need it," Larry said. "We need to keep that battery fresh."

Neil flicked off the light and continued to walk sideways, the walls actually growing closer and closer together. He could hear Larry coming behind him.

"I think we need to

go back," Neil said, feeling his ribs beginning to hurt.

"Is there still a breeze?"

Neil stopped and felt the cool air on his cheek. "Yes."

"Then this has to be the way. It must get wider again. Don't worry."

Worrying was exactly what Neil was doing now, with panic not far behind.

But he stepped and stepped and stepped. And then he stepped on something hard. It made a scraping sound, and he slid it a bit with his foot.

"That sounds like metal," Larry called.

Neil turned on the light, barely able to bend his arm enough to shine it down at the ground. He could tilt his head a bit to look down. There, at his feet, was a rusted and grime-covered skillet.

"It's the skillet!" he said.

"Can you get it?"

Neil tried a variety of ways to lift it, move it, or even push it.

"No. I can't bend down. I'm trying to kick it forward, but it's like it's jammed between the rocks. I can't flip it up, either."

"Okay, you keep going. I'll think of something."

"You sure?"

"Hey. I'm thinking like a bat, okay? I'll be fine. Just get a move on."

Neil turned off the light and kept moving forward. He now had to keep his legs completely straight to prevent his knees from banging against rock. If it got any narrower, he'd be stuck. Only the continued breeze kept him from losing hope.

He could hear grunts and other noises from behind him.

"Larry? You okay?"

Larry didn't answer, but Neil could still hear him making noise. Neil debated trying to slide back to help, but he took one more step. His leg emerged into open air. He could bend his knee and kick around without hitting rock.

"I'm through!" he called back.

Larry grunted.

Neil kept going. He stepped onto solid rock. He turned on the light and shone it around. He was in a large cavern, enormous, in fact. The ceiling was covered with thousands of sleeping bats.

Neil shone the light back at the crack.

"Larry? You okay?"

"Almost there."

There was something weird about Larry's voice. Like he was in pain.

"I'm coming back to help!" Neil said. He turned off the light and started to sidle back.

"No. No," Larry said. "Out. Of. Way."

Neil stepped back out and waited. He could hear Larry shuffling, puffing, and wheezing. Why was he having a harder time than Neil?

"No, I'm coming back!"

Just then Larry appeared, upside down. He was using his fingers to "walk." His face was squished sideways and his right cheek was scraped and bleeding.

He came out of the crack and toppled over, feetfirst, landing with a thud on the rock. In his right hand he was holding the rusty skillet.

CHAPTER THIRTY-SIX

MINE ALL MINE

Larry sat against the wall, his eyes rolling around in his head. "That was one major head rush," he said. "And not in a good way."

"You're an idiot," Neil said. "What if you'd blacked out? You'd be trapped in there."

"Hey, you told me to think like a bat. Bats hang upside down. I just took a couple of steps back and then flipped. The skillet was kind of jammed in sideways, but it was easy to get it unstuck once I could use my hands."

"Why didn't you go back and flip over again?"

"Flipping the first time was harder than it sounds. I almost busted my mouth." He grabbed his lower jaw in his hands and slid it from side to side. "Still works."

"Great. How about your brain?"

"Plus, I knew you'd found the exit, so I just kept going."

They looked at the skillet and then at each other.

"So, is there a hole in the middle?" Neil asked.

"Everything I'm looking at is spinning right now. You check."

Neil grabbed his shirtsleeve and began rubbing the surface of the metal. Layers of gunk and rust flaked off, revealing, in the almost dead center of the skillet, a small but recognizable hole.

"Feleena's story is true."

"Looks like it," Larry said, blinking. "But I see four bullet holes, swimming all around."

"Maybe if I smack you on the head with it, things will get clearer?"

"It's weird," Larry said. "There's no way that skillet could have been dropped by accident back there. It was rock, so Guillermo would have heard it. And if he went inside with the thing strapped to him, he would have noticed if it fell."

"Maybe it fell off and he couldn't pick it up. Just like me."

"Then why not say that?"

Neil examined the handle of the skillet. There was the rotted remnant of a leather strap tied around the end. Both ends of it were clean, like his rope had been in the canyon cave.

"It didn't fall off. He cut it off."

"Why?"

Neil held the skillet in his hands. It was cast iron,

thick, and heavy. He could imagine what it was like for Guillermo trying to squeeze through the crack. He'd been exhausted, carrying all that gold. "It was extra weight," Neil said. "Instead of getting rid of the gold, he cut this loose."

"He chose the gold over his mother's gift to him."

Neil nodded. "I don't think he realized until later what a horrible choice that was. So he changed the story for his ancestors."

"You're saying that a chef realized that there are more important things in life than money and success?" Larry smiled at Neil.

"Yeah. I guess that is what I'm saying."

"So, are we close to the actual exit?"

"I think so. There's a natural staircase up the back of the cave over there, and the breeze is pretty strong. I can also smell the creosote coming in from outside."

"Lovely." Larry stretched out on the rocks and closed his eyes.

"Wait, what are you doing?"

Larry pointed at the ceiling. "Thinking like a bat and getting some sleep." He almost immediately began snoring.

Neil stared at the skillet and the stairs to the exit. There was no way anyone could get in through the crack without him hearing. The exit was, according to Guillermo's legend, well hidden in the middle of a plateau. He was exhausted too. Exhilarated, but exhausted.

He lay down, holding the skillet tight, and closed his eyes, smiling. They'd done it. They'd found the mine. Despite all the danger, he and Larry had been successful.

Of course, it wasn't over yet.

Tomorrow they'd head outside.

They'd find an honest police force, maybe someone from an army base.

They'd show them the skillet, stake the claim, hand the money over to the Verdes . . . if they were still alive.

They'd avoid Aprende and Whippet, if they were still alive.

And then he'd finally be able to call home, to let everyone know he was okay.

And of course he'd also find out who the traitorous chef was, and show him or her what a real chef could do to an imposter.

Doing that well rested was going to be way easier than doing it in a walking coma. He turned off the cell phone and closed his eyes.

Within moments he was fast asleep.

Neil woke to the sound of a loud screeching shriek, like a scene from a horror movie. His ears were ringing. It was still dark and he fumbled for the skillet, sitting up and holding it in front of him.

He could hear swooping and diving all around the cave.

The bats.

They'd woken up and were swarming and flying around.

"That's the worst alarm clock ever," Larry yelled over the noise.

"I wonder what woke them up?"

"Are we alone?"

Neil crept down and shuffled close to the crack and smelled. He didn't sense anything or anyone different from yesterday. Certainly no one with old gunpowder The bats continued to screech and swoop.

"No one but us," Neil said.

"I have a theory, given my proven ability to think like a bat."

"What?"

"Insects. They come up after the rain ends. The bats are just having some breakfast."

"So it's morning?"

"Bats are nocturnal. I'm guessing it's closer to dawn."

"Let's get out of here and find out."

"Maybe your nose can find some eggs and we can use that skillet!"

Neil was afraid to see the swooping mass above him, so he turned on the light and pointed it at the ground, making his way to the stairway. Even still, he could see the bats swooping all around. It was like the shadows were alive.

"This is creepy," he said, gingerly stepping on the first level of the rock steps. "I wish they'd all just fly away."

"This is their home. We're the interlopers," Larry said, following him. "Just keep your head down and don't think about it. They don't want to hit us any more than we want to get hit."

The rock was slick, covered in centuries' worth of dripping minerals and, Larry pointed out, "other things."

"Be really careful not to get any of that in your mouth," Larry said. "It's got lots of dangerous stuff inside."

"Thanks for that image. I'll do my best."

They continued to climb.

"It's true," Larry said. "I read this story once about this poor girl who was looking up at the sky, and by a total statistical freak, some bird poop landed in her mouth. She spat it out but still got sick and died."

"I repeat, thanks for that image. Maybe if you close your mouth, you'll be safe."

"Yumnm, MMij," Larry mumbled.

Neil closed his mouth too and continued climbing. He could see a sliver of light peeking through the rock wall about twenty feet ahead of them. As he got closer, he could see bats flying in and out of a small hole. He pointed the phone ahead.

To reach the hole he'd have to make a leap from one pile of rocks to a narrow ledge underneath the opening. It wasn't a big distance, but if he missed, or slipped, he'd fall and land on the floor about a hundred feet below. He might survive, but he'd be totally beat up.

He turned and pointed to the gap. Then he mimed a jumping motion with his fingers.

Larry nodded.

Neil put the skillet down and rested the phone against it so that the light shone on the ledge on the other side of the gap.

Then he took a deep breath and jumped. His right foot landed on the ledge and his momentum slammed his face into the wall of the cave. He rebounded back and his left foot slipped and felt nothing but empty air.

Neil began frantically feeling for anything solid, waving his arms in a desperate attempt to find his footing and his balance. Bats flew past his head and out the hole.

"Your right foot is still on solid rock! Just lean forward," Larry yelled.

Neil did his best, despite his panic, to force his upper body forward. But he still felt like his body weight was pulling him back into the chasm.

"Don't let your butt go backward!"

Neil jerked his body and arms forward, using his right foot for balance. The motion pulled his point of gravity toward the wall. He banged his forehead on the rock, then pressed his body against the wall.

He put his left foot down and felt ground.

"Nice work!" Larry called, clapping. "You have a future in the circus."

"Thanks," Neil said. "When you get hired as a clown, you can tell them about me."

The hole was now just above him. He stuck his head through and could see rays of weak sunlight streaking across the sky. The bats hovered around the outside, avoiding the strange red-haired muddy blob that had invaded their back door. All he had to do was reach up and grab the edge and he could pull himself through.

He turned and waved to Larry. "Throw me the skillet, gently."

Larry held the skillet and counted, "One, two, three" as he swung it slowly, gauging the right weight. Luckily, he and Neil had done this many times in the kitchen with pots and pans in the middle of a crazy dinner

service, so he wasn't worried they'd drop it. He tossed it in the air toward Neil.

Neil held out both hands and cradled the skillet perfectly. He set it down on the ledge.

"All right, jump and I'll catch you."

Larry stood up and shook his head. "That's a perfect way to get us both killed. That ledge isn't big enough. Or we'll end up knocking that skillet down the hole and waste this entire trip."

"So what should I do?"

"Grab that skillet and get outside through the hole. I'll jump and then follow you."

Neil looked out the hole. He sniffed. There was the smell of creosote as well as damp dirt, poop, and cactus but nothing else out of the ordinary.

"All right, but if you fall, I'm coming to get you, treasure or no treasure."

"Fine."

Neil grabbed the skillet and reached up into the hole. He pulled himself up. "I feel like a gopher," he called back.

"From this end you look like a giant brown rutabaga."

Neil squeezed his head through. The sunlight warmed his face. He could see an eagle soaring in the distant sky. The coast seemed to be clear. He pulled up the skillet and slid it a few feet away. Then he bent his elbows and pulled himself through.

He leaned down and stuck his head back inside the hole. He could lean in just far enough to see Larry getting ready to leap.

"I'm out," he called.

At that moment the light from the phone shut off.

Larry actually laughed. "Ladies and gentlemen, as if the great Lare-dini were not brave enough, he will now attempt to leap across the chasm of death in TOTAL DARKNESS!" He gave himself a huge cheer.

"Don't!" Neil yelled. "Wait, I'm coming down. I'll grab the phone and recharge it!"

"No need." Larry began making loud clicking noises and then jumped. He landed square in the middle of the ledge, right below Neil's head. He barely had to move to keep his balance.

"Um . . . wow!" Neil said. "You never cease to amaze me, cuz."

Larry bowed.

"But why were you making that clicking sound?"

"Echolocation." Larry smiled. "We bats love it."

Larry grabbed Neil's arms and pulled him through. They sat down on the ground and gave long, satisfied sighs.

Neil took a look at his cousin, now that he could see him clearly in the sunlight. He was caked in dried mud, blood, and dust.

"What are you laughing at?" Larry said.

"We look, and smell, like giant balls of—"

"Don't say it. I know exactly what you mean."

Neil sniffed his armpit and gagged. "We should find a creek somewhere to wash up."

"No way. This is the best camouflage we could have." Larry stood up and dusted himself off, getting even messier. "All right, that's useless. But let's start moving."

"Which way?"

Larry pointed south. "We need to find a town or city fast."

Neil peered at the horizon. In the far distance was a ribbon of asphalt, with power lines running alongside the highway.

"Follow the electricity and we'll find people. And where we find people, let's hope we find someone friendly who'll listen to our side of the story."

CHAPTER THIRTY-SEVEN

NOT OK

They followed the highway closely but stayed far enough away that no one in a passing car would see them. The crust of brown was, as Larry predicted, a perfect cover, and they ducked down every time they heard any car approaching.

"Why don't we just turn on your phone and have someone find us?" Neil asked, his mouth feeling dry and cracked.

"We want to find someone, not have Aprende find us."

"Is it charged up?"

Larry pulled it out of his pocket and shook his head. "Not yet. That charger you bought stinks. I want my money back."

"You can go get your picture taken with Tammy. And just so you know, she's armed."

"On second thought, the charger is fine. Just a little slow."

He slid the phone back in his pocket.

"Okay, the sun is starting to go down. And the traffic

is getting more regular," Neil said. "I'm thinking we are approaching someplace densely populated."

"I wonder what sprawling metropolis awaits us."

"There's a sign up ahead," Neil said.

As they got closer, he began to shake. A severe man with a black cowboy hat, a six-shooter, a mustache, and a black cloak stared at them from the billboard.

"Please tell me that's not who I think it is," Neil said.

"It's not. Although in a way, it kind of is. That's Wyatt Earp. The guy Aprende wishes he was."

"Wyatt who?"

"Earp. He was a cop in a place called Tombstone. It was a lawless mining town, and he sort of kept the law any way he wanted to. He was a mix of hero and villain. And he was part of the famous shootout at the OK Corral."

Neil stared at the man, who stared back. "I heard something about that. There was a duel or something."

"Earp and his brother and a guy named Doc Holliday shot and killed some cowboys who'd tried to ambush them. It was one of those law versus outlaw in a lawless Old West boomtown things. At least, that's one version of the story."

"So we're heading to Tombstone?"

"Seems kind of fitting, pardner," Larry said with a drawl.

Neil couldn't take his eyes off the man on the sign, whose eyes seemed to follow him as he walked down the side of the road. Neil felt a wave of relief as they finally passed by.

The sun had now set, and they could see the faint glow of streetlights a few more miles away.

"So, do we walk in like this? Or wait until morning?" Larry asked.

Neil's lips were so dry they felt like they were going to crack. "I need a drink or I'm going to collapse."

"Tonight it is. We'll sidle up to the bar at the local watering hole and order us some sarsaparilla."

"With what? I used all the money we brought to buy the drone."

Larry grinned and pulled a tiny nugget of gold from his pocket.

They approached from the west. They walked down the main street, which was covered in dust. Old wooden buildings lined both sides, with signs out front that said SALOON, JAIL, MARSHAL'S OFFICE, and COURTHOUSE.

"I think I hear horses," Neil said. Sure enough, a horse-drawn carriage turned a corner and passed by them. The cowboy driver tipped his hat at Neil and Larry but continued on his way. His wagon was filled with barrels labeled GUNPOWDER and WHISKY XXXXX.

Neil caught a whiff of the gunpowder. Definitely filled with the same kind of saltpeter he'd smelled in Aprende's guns.

"This isn't good. I won't be able to tell if Aprende is anywhere near. Everything here smells like him."

A man and woman dressed in cowboy clothes walked down the wooden planked sidewalks.

"Did we pass through some kind of weird time portal back in the cave?" Neil said.

"I'm pretty sure that billboard we passed, and the streetlights, and the flashing neon 'we're open' sign on that saloon over there are modern."

"Open?" Neil said, smacking his lips.

"Let's say me and you mosey on over to yonder saloon and see what happens. At the very least there will be a lot of people around. If Aprende does show up and shoot us, we'll have witnesses."

They walked across the street and into a bar. Larry pushed the swinging saloon doors aside and walked through.

"I have *always* wanted to do that," Larry said as the doors swung back and forth on their hinges.

The tourists and bar patrons stared at them as they approached the bar.

Larry swung a foot onto the bar's brass foot rail and slammed his palm on the bar. "A coffee for me and a glass of milk for my friend here."

The bartender crossed her arms and frowned.

"What?" Larry said. "Ain't you never seen such pretty faces on a gold miner before?"

A group of tourists got up and circled around the scene. One or two began snapping pictures.

Neil instinctively drew closer to Larry and clutched the skillet handle. "Maybe we should leave?"

"They think we're part of the show," Larry whispered. "Let's go with it."

The woman continued frowning at Larry and even blew a large bubble with her gum, then snapped it.

Larry thumped the bar even harder. "We've been crawling through the desert, dodging scorpions, desperadoes, and coyotes for days. We may look and smell like the rear end of a donkey, but we are legit."

"Are you actually trying to order a drink?" the bartender said, looking even less impressed.

"Yes, ma'am. And I can pay, with this." He pulled the nugget out of his pocket and set it on the counter.

The bartender, who had probably seen more painted rocks than actual gold in her life, just stared.

"It's real," Larry said.

The bartender ran her fingers over the nugget, and

then stared at Larry and smiled. "It *is* real. This is worth a fortune!"

"Drinks for everyone, including you, my fair prairie flower. Keep the change."

The bartender was now all smiles and manners, and she handed Larry a giant mug of coffee. Larry drained it and then slammed the mug back down on the bar. "Keep it coming."

The tourists snapped more pictures. More and more came in through the saloon doors.

Neil wanted to jump behind the bar and crawl away, but Larry was clearly loving every moment.

Larry jumped up onto the bar. "That's right! We have struck it rich. And we are here to tell you that things are going to change round these parts. I want to speak to your mayor, and your marshal."

No one moved. They just snapped more pictures and crowded the bar for their free drinks.

Larry leaned down. "Why aren't they getting the authorities?"

"They still think this is part of the show," Neil said.

"I've been laying on the act a little too much?"

"Yeah. And I'm also willing to bet if we get shot, they'll think that's part of the show too, so time for plan B."

"Okay, get up here with me." Larry held his hand out and helped Neil up onto the bar.

Larry waved everyone to be quiet. "Okay, look. Listen, everyone. This isn't a show. The gold is real and we do need your help. There's a crazy sheriff who's trying to kill us, me and my cousin. He thinks we tried to kill someone."

Neil heard a gasp from behind her. The bartender had her hand over her mouth. "Oh my gosh! You're those two from the story in the newspaper! She pointed to a poster that hung over the bar. Poorly drawn pictures of Neil's and Larry's faces accompanied the words.

WANTED

DEAD OR ALIVE

REWARD FOR THEIR CAPTURE

$100,000

Larry's face broke out in a huge grin. "Can I have that?"

The bartender nodded happily, then took a picture of herself holding the sign in front of Neil and Larry. "I'm posting this right now. My friends are gonna freak!"

Larry smiled and nodded at Neil. "All according to plan."

Neil gave a nervous grin but kept clutching the skillet.

Larry held up the poster to the crowd. "Okay, you can all split the reward, but don't call the number on this poster. We need to speak to *your* marshal."

The bartender tapped Neil on the leg. "They can't help you. Most of them are here on a tour from Estonia. But I'll call the sheriff right now. She's my cousin, Dale."

"Um, thanks, I think," Neil said. "Help is on the way," he whispered to Larry.

"All right, everyone. Thanks, and remember that the drinks are still on the house. Slappy here and I are just gonna sit a spell, sip our drinks, and wait for the law." He began to climb down from the bar when a gravelly voice rang out from the back of the saloon.

"Move one more muscle and you are done for." All heads turned toward the voice.

Neil watched in horror as the back doors of the saloon swung open. Aprende limped through, his face a twisted scowl. His right arm was in a sling, his left was holding his six-shooter.

"*Erif Earp!*" a young boy yelled, pointing at Aprende. "*Jahtuma!*"

Everyone turned and gave out a long "Ooooohhhhhhhh." They began taking pictures of Aprende, laughing and repeating the phrase. "*Erif! Erif! Tulistage! Tulevahetus!*"

"What are they saying?" Neil asked.

Larry leaned in close. "I only know a little bit of Estonian, but I think they're saying, 'Shoot.'"

"Great."

"There're a lot of people between us and Aprende. If we jump down now, we can slip out the back."

They heard a sound

behind them and turned. The bartender was aiming a pistol at their backs. "You two ain't going anywhere until I get my reward."

"And I thought we were friends," Larry said. "You can forget about the tip."

"Drop it," said a voice from the back door.

"I really hope that's the marshal, and not who I think it is," Neil said.

He groaned as Whippet walked in, pointing a rifle at the woman and ordering her to drop the pistol. She did and then held her hands in the air, walking back toward the cash register. "I don't have much money," she said.

Whippet sneered. "I've got bigger fish to fry, honey."

Just then there was a loud crack from the back of the saloon, and Neil and Larry flinched. Neil checked his shirt for any signs of blood.

"What was that?"

Larry pointed at a hole in the ceiling. "I think the crowd is getting on Aprende's nerves."

Aprende was being crowded by the tourists. "Get away from me or the next bullet goes straight into the nearest one of ya," he yelled. The flashes from their cameras were blinding him, and he was pointing the gun all over the place.

"This might be our chance, pardner," Larry said, turning to Neil.

Neil nodded. "Red Herring on three?"

"With some soccer to 'em."

"One, two, three."

On three, Larry turned around and swung his leg with his best soccer kick. The force knocked the gun out of Whippet's hands. Neil swung the skillet and cracked Whippet on the side of the head, sending him crashing to the floor.

Aprende was still wrestling with the tourists, who were continuously snapping pictures. He pulled the trigger again and a bullet crashed into the mirror behind the bar. Shards of glass rained down on Whippet and the bartender.

"Now!" Neil yelled.

He and Larry jumped down from the bar and scurried out the side door.

Larry turned back and yelled, "If your cousin gets here, tell her we need help!"

"What about the REWARD?" she yelled, cowering down behind the bar. Whippet was stumbling to his feet next to her.

"I promise, if we don't end up dead, you'll get more than your share!"

She smiled, then turned and smashed a bottle over Whippet's head.

"I like her," Larry said as he and Neil ran down a back alley.

There was another gunshot and then the screams of dozens of panicked tourists. "I think they just realized this isn't an act," Larry said.

Neil ran faster. They slipped out and turned right to go down another back lane. A bullet shattered the brick above Neil's head.

"The new marshal or the old?" Larry asked.

Neil sniffed bat guano. "Aprende. Keep running."

The lane ended in a parking lot. There was another

shot and they ran across the lot, ducking behind cars.

They slipped past a minivan and then hopped a fence.

"Is this a miniature golf course?" Neil asked as he almost smashed into the wooden cutout of a waving cowboy.

"Nothing says 'Old West' quite like it."

They heard Aprende's voice yell across the lot. "In the name of the law, I command that you stop and surrender."

"Why is he yelling that?" Neil asked as they hopped the other fence. "He knows we're not going to stop."

"He's making sure that any witnesses will testify that we were trying to escape."

Aprende fired again and the bullet rang like a bell off the metal bar of the fence.

"That was way too close," Neil said. They ran into another alley. On one side was a high wall, and on the other was the brick exterior of a large building. They could see the main road past the opening at the end. Tourists were running as fast as they could, away from something.

"What the heck?" Larry said.

The last tourist disappeared, and Neil saw Whippet come into view. He was limping and holding his rifle in front of him.

"Quick, over the wall!" Larry said.

Whippet turned and saw them. He raised his rifle and fired, just as Neil and Larry reached the top of the wall. The bullet cracked the brick at Neil's feet, but he and Larry swung themselves over to the other side and landed with a thud.

Larry got up first and looked at the wall. There was a

huge oak door that led back where they came from. Larry pushed on it and it didn't budge.

"Good. There's no way two limping loonies are going to be able to climb in here."

Neil rubbed his shoulder, then looked around. They were in the middle of a completely open courtyard, with a brick wall on three sides, and the wall of a large brick building at the other end.

And in the middle stood a large wooden platform. Steps led up to a scaffold, and there, swaying in the wind, were two nooses.

"What?" Larry said, seeing the expression on Neil's face. He followed his cousin's gaze. "That's disturbing."

The ropes creaked as they moved in the moonlight. The sight was both hypnotic and frightening.

"We've got to get out of here." Neil got up and walked around the edge of the wall, keeping as much distance between himself and the scaffold as he could.

"Don't be such a fraidy cat," Larry said. He climbed up onto the scaffold and slapped the rope. "This is probably the gallows for the local jail. That building at the other end."

"It gives me the creeps."

"The *old* jail. The one from the OK Corral days." Larry jumped up and down on the trapdoor that stood under the noose. "See, the platform doesn't even work. It's a prop."

"Just get away from there, okay?"

"Fine. But we should try to find someplace to hide."

"I thought you said they couldn't get over the wall."

"They can't. But there has to be some door somewhere in the jail building where they brought in the prisoners for hanging. We need to head out before they can head in."

"What's that big door you just pushed?"

"That was where the coroner would come in with his carriage to take the bodies away."

"Nice."

"What we need to find is the door that leads from the prison cells to the courtyard. It's got to be over there at the far end."

"Okay." Neil continued feeling his way around the wall. His shoulder bumped against something hard and metal. "I think I found a hinge."

Larry jumped off the scaffold and walked over. "Good job. Okay, let's figure out a way to get this door opened."

Neil could hear angry voices from the other side of the brick wall and oak door.

"You stay here and shoot them if they try to come back over," said Aprende.

Whippet responded, but Neil couldn't hear what he said.

"We'll get you to a doctor as soon as we get those two. That skillet he conked you with is worth millions, and I'm not leaving here without it."

Neil looked at the gallows. "Let's hurry."

Larry and Neil felt around the door, but it was locked

from the other side. "What about the window?" Neil asked.

There was a small window with a metal grille bolted on top of it.

"Nope. Too small and also too far up to reach in and grab the lock, even if we could get that grille off."

"So, we're trapped," Neil said.

Larry tapped the door. "Wait, this is old technology."

"Meaning?"

"Hand me the skillet, chef boy."

Neil handed Larry the skillet. Larry got down on his knees and held the skillet flat against the bottom hinge. Then he slid it up quickly. A metal pin flew in the air, and Larry caught it before it could hit the ground. He held it up to Neil.

"This little pin holds the two parts of the hinge together." He patted the skillet. "Finesse is almost always better than brute force. And now for the top hinge."

He did the same thing on the top hinge, and that pin flew out as well.

"Now we grab that grille and pull."

Neil and Larry grabbed the metal and yanked. The door was stuck fast, but the more they wiggled, the more it started to move. Finally, with one big heave, they swung it open, the lock cracking.

The heavy door crashed to the ground.

"Let's go!" Larry said.

They ran inside. To their right was a large room filled with old mining equipment, including shovels, lamps, and picks. It was all against the walls. "There's nowhere to hide in there," Neil said.

They heard the sound of breaking glass from the front of the building. A flashlight shone inside, and they ducked. There were more smashing noises and the ding of metal being hit with something hard.

"He's trying to break the lock," Neil said.

"Upstairs," Larry said. They crawled along the floor to the stairs, then bolted up three at a time. There was an old library at the top of the stairs, but it was completely exposed.

They turned right and ran into an old courtroom. Everything was polished wood, but apart from the judge's bench, there was nowhere to hide.

"This is no good," Neil said. "We're doomed."

They could hear footsteps below, shuffling toward the open door. Aprende kicked something, which broke, then walked out into the courtyard.

Neil peeked out a window and saw him walk to the middle of the courtyard and look around. Then he called something out to Whippet. Aprende took out his gun and then marched back toward the building.

"He's coming."

"There's one more room at the front," Larry said. A sign over the top read PIONEER ROOM.

They hurried inside. "This is more like it!" Larry said.

Lining the front of the room was a half wall. Old leather saddles hung from hooks on the display. Behind those were two large and, as Larry put it, "very breakable windows."

The side walls carried displays about life in the time of the earliest western settlers, including lots of old guns, rifles, and even ceremonial swords and knives. There were also dummies dressed in period clothes.

The footsteps downstairs returned from outside and they could hear Aprende cursing. Whippet's voice came from the front entrance.

"I don't care how dizzy you feel. You stay there and keep watch," Aprende yelled. "I'm going upstairs. Shoot anything that comes out."

Larry ducked behind the wall with the saddles. "Neil, get over here!"

Aprende's footsteps sounded on the wooden stairs.

He stopped. "Wait. I have a better plan."

Neil slipped off his shoes. A horrible smell rose to his nose and he fought the urge to gag. He picked up his shoes, then slid quietly in his socks over to the display of pioneer clothes. He stood between the man and woman, holding the skillet behind his back. All he had to do was wait for Aprende to walk in, and then he could bring down the skillet on his head.

He made eye contact with Larry, who nodded and then ducked back down behind the wall.

Aprende walked into the courtroom first, upending displays and knocking over chairs and tables. He did the same in the other rooms, before finally shuffling toward the Pioneer Room.

"Well, well. It ends here, I guess," Aprende said. "I've grown impressed by you two boys. It's not anyone who can stand up to Joe Aprende and live to talk about it. Of course, you won't live to talk about it."

He cocked his gun but didn't walk into the room.

Neil fought a sense of panic. What was he doing? Why wasn't he coming in? Neil's hands began to sweat, and he fought to keep his grip on the skillet.

Aprende moved some furniture around in the hallway. Then there was the sound of paper being ripped from the books in the library.

"About forty years ago, when I was just a kid, I almost had that map. Well, my little brother and me, that is. Old Mr. Verde used to keep it in a box, and he showed it to me once, when I was delivering groceries to his ranch. That was before he had any idea who I was. I came back that same night and broke inside. The box was just kept there on the mantelpiece. The map to the mine his family stole from us."

There was more ripping paper and more shuffling of furniture.

"We almost got caught. That little Julio had ears like an elephant and we got out just before his dad came rushing into the room. We hid in the barn while everyone was searching. Then I had a great idea. We'd destroy the farm and any evidence that we were ever there. The hay in the barn was so dry it hardly took any time at all to spark up a proper fire. I figured the sparks would take out the main house too, but then the wind changed all of a sudden."

Neil heard Aprende throwing something around. He saw a book slide across the floor at his feet.

"I almost died in that fire. I did suffer burns to my face, but we jumped out and ran. That's the only way out of a burning building, jumping. Of course, my idiot brother panicked when he saw the flames and dropped the box with the map. I'd assumed it was destroyed, until my friend Mary Maize told me about this festival, and the ghost story, and the search for the lost mine."

Neil could hear the sound of Aprende striking a match. He smelled the sulfur first and then the unmistakable smell of burning paper.

"So, now you have a choice. I'll stay out here just long enough to make sure you can't come out this way. If you try, I'll put a bullet through you. If you don't, you'll burn. If you try to jump out the window, my brother will shoot you. Everyone knows you two are desperate outlaws, so no one will question us."

"I wouldn't be so sure about that," Larry called.

Aprende fired at the wall. The bullet went through the flimsy plaster and shattered the window.

"Missed!" Larry said.

"Keep talking," Aprende said. He fired another bullet a few feet to the right. It also passed through, shattering the other window.

Neil had no way of knowing if Larry was far from, or close to, the bullets, but as long as they went through without stopping, he assumed Larry hadn't been hit.

"Just thought you should know," Larry called out, "that I just recorded your whole speech and posted it on the Internet. The audio isn't the greatest, but beggars can't be choosers."

Aprende began firing wildly, yelling. The bullets tore through the wall again and again.

The shooting stopped, and Neil could hear Larry moaning in pain. He was about to leap out to help him when he saw Aprende walk into the room, smoke billowing around him. He was reloading his pistol, his eyes locked on the walls. He lifted the gun and prepared to fire again.

Neil waited until he was just a step away, then leaped out with the frying pan, ready to smash Aprende on the head.

Larry's voice came out loud and clear.

"Duck!"

Neil threw himself to the floor just as Aprende turned around and fired.

Neil saw Aprende stare down at his own chest and then stumble back.

"I told you to stay downstairs," Aprende said.

Neil looked into the doorway. Whippet was standing behind the pile of burning books, his own shirt now spreading with crimson. "I thought I saw someone coming upstairs after you, so I followed. I'm so . . ." He dropped his rifle and reached out toward his brother. Then his eyes fluttered and he fell back.

The flames grew higher and higher.

Aprende was as white as a ghost. His pistol fell from his fingertips and landed on the floor. Neil shoved it away, then stood up and ran to the wall.

Neil leaned over. Larry was lying on the ground, bleeding. He was holding one of the saddles in front of his head and chest. Four bullets were lodged into the thick leather.

"Old technology," Larry coughed. Then he held up his cell phone. "And new technology. Together they save the day." Then he fell back and passed out.

Neil looked at the wounds. Most were minor, but one hole in Larry's leg looked serious. He grabbed a strap from the saddle and tightened it around Larry's thigh, making it as tight as he could. He turned around. The fire was now blazing. There was only one way out. He lifted Larry and walked to the shattered window.

There was a porch roof outside, and Neil stepped out into the cool evening air. A searchlight scanned the front of the courthouse, and Neil had to squint to see what was happening below. There were sirens and flashing lights.

A fire engine pulled up. Firefighters streamed into the front door and a ladder was being raised toward the roof.

He saw a police car with the lights flashing. The bartender was next to her cousin the sheriff, pointing up. She focused the light on Neil.

He heard the squawk of a megaphone being turned on.

"Stay there. No one else needs to get hurt."

Neil nodded as clearly as he could. "I'm unarmed," he yelled. He tried to concentrate on Larry's breathing, willing him to stay strong.

The ladder banged against the stone railing of the porch and a firefighter sped up toward Neil.

Neil handed Larry to him and then climbed down. An ambulance arrived, and paramedics quickly loaded Larry inside.

Larry woke and gave Neil a thumbs-up, then fell back on his stretcher.

Neil smiled, choking back tears.

"I'm afraid you can't go with him," the sheriff said. She grabbed Neil by the wrists and handcuffed him, then pushed him into the back of her squad car.

He watched as the ambulance sped away.

The bartender opened the passenger door and sat in the front seat.

"The hospital isn't far," she said. "My cousin talked to the paramedics. Your friend's gonna be okay."

"Cousin."

"Oh. Your cousin is going to be okay, then. That's what she says anyway. I might even go visit him after we drop you off at the jail. My cousin says she needs to arrest him, too. So, you know, I might tag along."

Neil shook his head. "Take him a coffee. He'll like that."

"Thanks!"

Despite his tears, Neil couldn't help but chuckle.

CHAPTER THIRTY-EIGHT

SURPRISE, ARIZONA

Neil could feel someone poking at him as he lay on the hard cot in the jail cell. He had to fight the grogginess as the face of the sheriff swam into view. He felt like he had just fallen asleep.

"Wake up, sir. You're free to go."

Neil wiped the sleep from his eyes and stared up at the sheriff. "What?"

"I said you're free to go, sir. And there's someone waiting for you in the holding pen."

Neil could smell Isabella's lavender perfume. He leaped up and rushed through the open cell door and into the waiting room.

It wasn't Isabella.

Feleena was sitting on a bench, wearing Isabella Tortellini perfume. She was alive!

She rushed over and gave Neil a huge hug. Tears were pouring down her face. "My father and I cannot thank you enough. You have saved us."

She let go and stepped back, wiping her eyes on the sleeves of her jean jacket.

Neil was confused. "I'm so . . . happy, but . . . wait . . . I thought you got shot."

Feleena nodded, laughing and crying. "Aprende and Whippet came to see us. They demanded we tell them where you were. My father refused. We didn't care anymore. They needed to be stopped. Aprende shot my father in the leg. He said it was a warning. Then he shot me in the arm." She raised her sleeve, and Neil could see her left arm was heavily bandaged.

The sheriff came out from behind her desk and handed Neil a plastic bag. Inside was the map, now horribly crumpled, some loose change, and his wallet. "Oh, and this, of course," she said, pulling the skillet out of a drawer and handing it to Neil.

"I think this belongs to Feleena," Neil said, handing her the skillet. "And with it, everything in the mine."

Feleena took it like she was being handed a delicate egg. Then she shook her head and handed it back to Neil. "You keep it. We will all *share* in the riches of the mine, but you showed the skill necessary to find it. I think Guillermo would be happy to see this special memorial given to someone who can appreciate its true value."

Neil bowed. "I feel like Guillermo was watching over us the whole time. The weather, the weird good luck sometimes. Whatever Whippet thought he saw in the courthouse."

Feleena looked at Neil with a sideways glance. "You don't believe in ghosts, do you?"

Neil smiled and shrugged. "The world has more in it than is dreamed of in your philosophy," he said.

"Is that Shakespeare?"

Neil nodded. "Larry says it's his favorite line. From *Ham Cutlet,* or whatever the play is called."

"*Hamlet,*" Feleena said, smiling.

"How is Larry?"

"He is well."

Neil beamed.

"All the people on the floor of the hospital seem to love him. They all keep bringing him free coffees."

"That's my cousin," Neil said. "Did he mention that we had to make some promises to a few people along the way to get help?"

Feleena nodded. "Yes. I have a list. Selma the architect. Anna the guide."

"Anna's alive!"

"Yes. Apparently she was hiding, as she told you. Chef Hayes saw her donkey wandering alone and followed it up the paths. Then he saw Aprende following you. He followed too."

"Then he followed Aprende and Whippet into the desert?"

She nodded. "He saved your life. He was able to escape in the dust storm, and then found Anna waiting for him when he got back to the canyon."

"He also gave me the recipe that unlocked the map. I hope he's on your list too."

Feleena nodded. "Definitely. There is also the bartender from the saloon, and apparently the Estonian tour guide service and anyone on the 'Come See Tombstone' tour. And the courthouse was damaged, but not destroyed, and my father and would like to pay to have that restored as well."

Neil laughed. "I hope there's some left for the ranch!"

"From what Larry tells us, there is a *lot* of gold in that mine. We have enough to save the ranch and to keep the festival going and to do so much more. Guillermo and Rosita, and my mother, would be so proud."

"What about Chef Maize? Aprende called her a 'friend.'"

"She disappeared the same day Aprende came to attack us. She is either hiding, or Aprende saw her as one more loose end to get rid of."

Neil gave a deep sigh. "Feleena, I am so happy that this worked out, but I am so exhausted. I just want to go home."

"The hospital says Larry will need a few days to recover and then you can travel. I will drop you off there on my way back home. My father is back at the ranch and would love to see you before you leave."

"I'd like to see the ranch one more time too." Neil turned to the sheriff. "Am I really free to go?"

"Yes. There won't be a trial. The audio your cousin

uploaded clears your name for almost everything. If you're going to be sticking around for a few days, I'll catch up with you to get your statement later, but I think your cousin gave us all the info we needed."

Neil walked over and shook her hand. "Thanks. I hope your cousin shares some of that reward with you."

"Oh, she will, you can be sure of that."

Neil turned to Feleena. "One last favor?"

"Of course, anything."

"Can I borrow your cell phone? I want to call some people."

As Feleena drove to the hospital, Neil sat in the passenger seat and dialed everyone back home. His parents didn't answer. Angel didn't answer. Sean Nakamura didn't answer. Neil had left Isabella for last, not wanting to feel rushed when he heard her voice. But she didn't answer either. He tried Jones, but there was no answer there.

Neil fought a rising sense of panic. His phone was long dead, but he could access his voice mail messages. He dialed the number and listened. His in-box was full.

He breathed a sigh of relief. His friends and family had been trying to reach him, and they were all just busy.

He pressed the play button. As the messages played, a chill ran down his spine.

A man's voice, with an accent he couldn't place, spoke softly, barely above a whisper.

"Neil Flambé. You do not know me, but I know you. I know you very well. I have seen what you have done to my friends. Now it is my turn to see what I can do to *your* friends."

Neil pressed play for the next message.

It was from Isabella's phone. He breathed a sigh of relief. But then the message was the same voice. "It's so cold where we are. I hope you can find us."

The next call was from Angel's phone, but again the same voice. "So very, very cold. You haven't even begun to look. You must hurry."

It was the same on all the other messages.

Then the last message, using up all the rest of the available memory, was the sound of crashing waves and shrieking birds.

Neil just stared at the phone.

"Neil, are you okay?" Feleena asked. "You look ill."

Neil raised his head. "I just need to make one more call." Neil dialed Larry's number and held the phone to his ear, a feeling of dread washing over him. Someone picked up, and Neil breathed.

"Ah, Neil Flambé. How nice of you to call. This makes a perfect baker's dozen."

"Who are you?" Neil yelled into the phone.

"It is so very, extremely cold where we are, Chef Flambé. Remember that. So. Very. Cold. Endurance is impossible."

Then the phone line went dead.

They arrived at the hospital. Neil bolted from the car and ran to the front desk.

"I'm here to see my cousin, Larry Flambé. Where is he?"

"He left," the nurse said. "He was transferred by a helicopter just a short time ago."

"Helicopter? Why?"

"He was dying."

Neil shook his head. "No, no, no, he wasn't. He'd been talking to people, making jokes, drinking coffee."

"Sometimes people's conditions can change rapidly. He was taken to the emergency room at the main hospital in Phoenix."

"Call them. Call them and see how he's doing. Please."

"Okay, okay." The nurse picked up the phone and dialed. She had a short conversation, then hung up. She looked at Neil, her eyes wide. "They say they have no record of anyone being admitted. I have the paperwork right here, but they say they never sent a helicopter . . . I'm sorry."

"Where was his room?!"

"Thirteen B."

Neil ran down the hallway and skidded to a stop in front of an open doorway. There on the pillow was a perfect replica of his own destroyed phone.

He stepped over, slowly reaching out for the phone.

As soon as he touched it, the phone buzzed.

Neil held it up. A text appeared from an unlisted number with the word *Ice*. He scrolled down and there was a photo of all his friends, frozen like statues, displayed on the top of a long dining table.

The photo disappeared and a new text appeared.

This time you'll have to do it all . . . alone.

Then the phone went dead.

Neil threw it against the wall, and it shattered into a dozen pieces.

ACKNOWLEDGMENTS

So many people help an author make a book, it's hard to fit them all into a small space like this. This might seem a bit like an Oscar speech.

But, obviously my Arizona-based family, friends, and colleagues top the list for thanks.

Doug, Anna and Darcy, and my Mum and Dad.

(And Tim and Betty who live in Buffalo, but we seem to get together in Arizona a lot!)

The Boyers, Fahys, and McClenahans—great friends and hosts.

The amazing crew at Changing Hands Bookstore and First Draft Book Bar. I could sit in either store for hours reading, sipping craft beer . . . and buying books!

And everyone back in the East too.

Ruta Rimas—editor extraordinaire. (She's also the kick-butt editor of my series *MiNRS*: Go check it out!)

Laurent Linn—who always makes my books look better (and has his own book coming out too . . . *buy it!*)

Kevin Hanson, Justin Chanda, and Jon Anderson—the bigwigs at Simon & Schuster who show me so much support.

The crew at Westwood Creative Artists—including my champion agent, Michael Levine.

And of course, the PR people at Simon & Schuster and Simon & Schuster Canada who make sure people know about my red-headed chef and his weird friends.

And last, but not least . . .

Laura, Erin, and Emily, who make everything fun.

Kevin Sylvester is an award-winning and best-selling writer, illustrator, and broadcaster.

This is the sixth book in his Neil Flambé Capers. He's always loved ghost stories and hopes one day to stumble on a lost gold mine.

His sci-fi series MiNRS is out now. Space. Check it out.

Kevin is also the writer and illustrator of *Super-Duper Monster Viewer*, *Baseballogy*, *Splinters*, *Gold Medal for Weird*, *Sports Hall of Weird*, *Follow Your Money*, and a lot of other books that he promises are fun!